He was so close, his ...

The voice coming from deep in his chest was pure, sensuous persuasion.

'I don't know, Thomas,' she whispered, meeting his gaze. 'I truly don't know.'

He ran his fingers down her cheek, his blood leaping at the feel of smooth, warm skin. Passion hardened his body, coiling low and deep and demanding. She made a sighing sound. Her lashes fluttered down as she lifted her face to his in soft surrender.

Thomas stilled, his body and mind clashing. The urge to take was maddeningly strong. But there was something else. His hand fell from her cheek.

'I think you should know whether or not you want me to stop. After all, we are adults,' he said matter-of-factly. 'I want you very much. I also want the feeling to be mutual. It's been a long day, so...good night, Katy...'

Dear Reader,

Great holiday reading *is* Silhouette Desire®—but even if you're not going away this month, there's always July's scorching novels to make you feel better! Lounge in the garden or by the pool with our MAN OF THE MONTH, Bryan Willard, from Lass Small's *The Coffeepot Inn*—absolute bliss!

Follow Trenton Laroquette's search for the right woman in *The Bride Wore Tie-Dye* by Pamela Ingrahm, and don't miss Beverly Barton's *The Tender Trap*—where an unplanned pregnancy prompts an unexpected proposal!

Talented award-winning author Jennifer Greene has created another seductive story with the second of the Stanford Sisters in *Bachelor Mum*, and there's something a little bit different from Ashley Summers, *On Wings of Love*.

The Loneliest Cowboy is Pamela Macaluso's charming story where the hero meets up with an old flame he can't even remember, so he gets the surprise of his life when he hears her long-kept secret!

Enjoy!

The Editors

On Wings of Love
ASHLEY SUMMERS

SILHOUETTE
Desire®

*Silhouette, Silhouette Desire and Colophon
are registered trademarks of Harlequin Books S.A.,
used under licence.*

*First published in Great Britain 1997
Silhouette Books, Eton House, 18-24 Paradise Road,
Richmond, Surrey TW9 1SR*

© Faye Ashley 1997

ISBN 0 373 76050 7

22-9707

*Printed and bound in Great Britain
by Mackays of Chatham PLC, Chatham*

ASHLEY SUMMERS

is an incurable romantic who lives in Texas, in a house that overflows with family and friends. Her busy life revolves around the man she married thirty years ago, her three children and her handsome grandson, Eric. Formerly the owner and operator of a landscaping firm, she enjoys biking, aerobics, reading and travelling.

Other novels by Ashley Summers

Silhouette Desire®

Fires of Memory
The Marrying Kind
Juliet
Heart's Delight
Eternally Eve
Heart's Ease

To Virginia and John McKinney
and my beloved niece, Terry Hartley

One

Katy Lawrence parked her car in the shade of an ancient apple tree and slowly got out. Oblivious to the gravel under her bare feet, she stared at the place that would be her home for the next five weeks. A chill of wonder went up her spine. The Victorian house, all sparkling white paint and lacy gingerbread trim, drowsed in the mists like a sweet, vague memory from the distant past. It was a most bewitchingly haunting feeling.

Keeping her gaze on the house, Katy found her sandals and slipped them on with only a quick downward glance. The mossy brick walkway leading to the front door was a perfect touch, she thought. She felt another feathery chill.

"For heaven's sake, it's just an old house, Katy," she chided herself. She was not usually given to whimsy.

She quickened her pace and mounted the steps, then crossed the veranda. Above the old-fashioned door knocker hung a hand-written sign that read, "Come on in, I'm around somewhere."

Hesitantly she opened the door and stepped into the cool, shadowed entryway. "Hello?" she called. "Hello, anyone home?"

No answer. She waited for a moment, then walked on. When she reached the living room, her peculiar sense of déjà vu deepened to tiny shocks of recognition.

Katy nibbled her lip as she gazed around the airy room. She had never seen this house before, yet each object her eyes encountered evoked the same puzzling sense of familiarity. The words *Of course!* sang through her mind. Of course there were lace curtains at the windows. Of course there were gleaming wooden floors, and the sensuous curves of wicker furniture stained the exact hue of sweet-clover honey. Even the fresh flowers were a given, as was the basket of green apples on the coffee table.

Three perfectly round, black-and-white stones lay beside them, luring her fingers to caress their water-smoothed surfaces. Resisting the urge to touch, she made another appraisal of the room with a travel writer's critical gaze. Since it was a bed and breakfast, not a hotel, she'd give the place three stars on first impression alone, Katy decided. Whoever lived here had a good eye for the small touches that made a house so welcoming to a traveler.

Who lived here? she wondered. This was a professional establishment, surely accustomed to the arrival of guests at some point during the afternoon. So where were the hosts?

Silence. The soft heat of an island summer drifted through the open windows, fragrant with the enticing scent of new-mown grass and the faint seawater tang of Puget Sound. Catching back the golden strands of hair tickling her cheeks, Katy eyed the tray sitting on a wicker table. It contained a pitcher of iced lemonade. For guests? Deciding it was, she poured a glass and drank it with hearty enjoyment.

Cold lemonade on a hot summer day. With a poignant sense of loss, Katy suddenly realized why this warm, elegantly time-worn room tugged at her heartstrings. It reminded her of her grandmother's house in Spokane.

"God, I haven't thought of Grammy in ages!" she whispered, shivering as the long-ago memory opened a tiny crack in the mental dam that had kept her safe. The specter of loss slipped through, and she was overcome with a frightening sense of vulnerability.

"No," Katy said, squaring her shoulders. She forced herself to focus on the photographs adorning the fireplace mantel. She studied them, her mouth softening. Children, parents and grandparents. Two young couples in various poses, with and without the children. A handsome teenager holding up a string of fish which, judging from the rod in his other hand, he had caught. Family, she thought, and felt the familiar pinch of longing.

Her gaze shot back to the young fisherman. Above the mantel was a large framed portrait of the same man. He appeared to be thirty or so at the time it was painted. His skin was tanned, his coal-black hair charmingly tousled. Her gaze stopped on his face, suddenly riveted as a sweet quill of feeling arrowed through her. He had a strong, aquiline nose and a stubborn chin. But it was his eyes that caught and held her attention. Those sky blue eyes seemed to be looking directly at her.

Entranced by the clarity of his gaze, Katy studied his face. There was something about his expression, an openness she found very pleasing.

She started as a sound broke her bemusement. Someone was whistling. Turning, she glanced through an interior doorway, past a golden-oak table and out a bank of windows that overlooked the back lawn. Behind the house lay a meadow. And striding through the lush green grass was the man in the picture.

Whistling as he walked, he swung a small metal bucket in each hand, brimful with ripe raspberries. He was dressed in a T-shirt, faded jeans and scruffy sneakers. Her breath caught, and she had to force herself to exhale. Even from this distance he was an arresting man.

Drawing herself up to her full height of five-feet-three and one-quarter inches, Katy took a step forward, only to stop in sudden indecision. Should she wait to be discovered or walk to meet him? And while she stood here and dithered, he swung lithely across the lawn and down the redwood deck to the screened door.

Katy reminded herself that she was twenty-nine and a little too old to be thrown by an attractive male. But damn, he was appealing! Ruggedly so, with the kind of muscles that came from hard work, not a gym.

She saw his vivid blue eyes widening as he stepped inside and saw her, then crinkle at the corners with a smile.

"Well, hello!" he said. "This is one of my nicer surprises today." He set down the buckets and stuck out his hand. "I'm Thomas Logan. And you are ... ?"

Katy started to shake hands, then realized she still held her empty glass. Putting it down, she slipped her hand into his hard, brown fingers.

"Katy Lawrence." She paused expectantly. "I've just arrived. On the ferry," she went on when he tipped his head quizzically. *Idiot! Of course you arrived on the ferry,* she chided herself silently. *How else could you get on and off the island? Except by plane—and you've just driven all the way from California to avoid flying.*

"Mr. Logan, I called and made reservations. For five weeks?" she prompted. "A woman answered the phone."

"That would be Maddie. She handles most reservations."

Who was Maddie? Katy reclaimed her hand, conscious of a tingling in her fingers. "Maddie? Is she the owner?"

"Maddie's the maid. I'm the owner."

Her eyebrows rose. "*You* run this B&B?"

"Yes. Shouldn't I?"

That quizzical smile shaped his mouth again.

Katy blushed, a maddening trait. "Yes, of course, I was just . . . Mr. Logan, do I have a room or not?"

"Yes, Miss Lawrence, you have a room." His voice deepened. "It is miss, isn't it?"

Rattled, she gave a brusque nod.

He relaxed into a grin that weakened her knees.

"Welcome to Tumbling Brook Farm, Miss Lawrence."

"Thank you. Is it a real farm?"

"No, not really, not anymore. But I liked the name, so I kept it." Pulling a red bandanna from his rear pocket, he wiped his damp forehead. "Warm out there! Where are you from?"

"Southern California. San Diego, to be exact."

"And you drove here?"

"Yes. I like to drive." Hearing the hint of defensiveness in her reply, Katy lifted her chin, her gaze a tad defiant.

Thomas turned away. "Well, you'll find this a very restful place, ideal for restorative purposes," he said lightly. "Your bags still in the car? Five weeks, you say?"

"Yes." Katy followed him out the door. "That's not a problem, is it?"

"Not at all."

He glanced back at her and she noted the laugh lines around his eyes and mouth. Mid-thirties, she decided. An experienced charmer, no doubt. Why hadn't she been told about him? Her friend, Patsy Palmer, lived on the island and had recommended Tumbling Brook Farm. But she hadn't mentioned its handsome owner.

All those telephone chats, Katy thought dryly, and not once had Thomas Logan's name come up. "That little minx!" she muttered wryly.

Thomas's long legs had already carried him to her car. She hurried past him and unlocked the trunk. Easily he lifted out the two large leather bags, leaving only a camera case and favorite pillow for her to carry.

Just as she reached inside the trunk for her things, Katy heard a sound that stiffened her slim body to a taut line. A small airplane flew overhead, its engine loud enough to hurt her ears. She stilled, mentally following its flight. She felt a scream welling up—the plane was too low, surely it was too low! She shuddered, struggling for control. But the sound swelled into a snarling roar that filled her entire being. Suddenly, reality vanished, and she was caught in a steely web of memory.

For a desolate moment, Katy felt powerless to free herself; the memory that froze her in place was crystal-clear. The combination of grief, horror and impotent rage was so strong she could taste its bitter tang...

"Miss Lawrence? Are you all right?"

The husky male voice had the effect of a soft touch on bare skin. There was incredible tenderness in it. Like splintering ice, the spell broke, and Katy let out the breath she'd been holding. A swift glance over her shoulder located Thomas standing at the edge of the driveway, waiting for her. Had he noticed her reaction to the plane? *Idiot! Of course he'd noticed.* Color scalded her cheeks as she met his concerned gaze.

Katy forced a laugh. "Yes, my goodness, of course I'm all right! It was just..." She inhaled, laughed again, shook her head at her foolishness. "I don't usually freak out when an airplane flies over, but this one was so loud. And so *low!*"

"Just a friend buzzing me. On his way to pick up a couple of tourists, I imagine," Thomas said. "I'm sorry it disturbed you."

"It just startled me. Let me get my camera and pillow, and I'll be right with you." She'd covered pretty well, Katy thought. She picked up her camera case. The sound of the plane had faded into the distance. The memory had faded, too, but it had left its calling card.

With practiced discipline, Katy drew a long, deep breath and stilled her inner trembling. Then she grabbed her pillow, closed the trunk and turned to face him with a bright smile. "Can't sleep without my special pillow! I've had it since college."

His deep chuckle sent a rush of warmth through her body. Katy stepped around him and led the way back up the mossy, brick walkway. Her gaze, circling the yard, was curious and eager. On one side, young pear trees held a bounty of miniature fruit. On the other, a well-tended bed of huge pink peonies backed by white daisies flowed along an old stone fence. Pots of pansies and sweet alyssum flanked the steps. An inviting white wicker swing graced the porch.

"Who's the gardener?" she asked.

"I am. It's a great way to forget your troubles."

What kind of troubles? Biting back the question that sprang to her lips, she stepped over a sleeping calico cat and preceded Thomas Logan to the door.

Once inside, he took the lead. The wide staircase rose to a windowed landing, turned sharply and continued to the second floor. He stopped before an open door and allowed her to enter the airy room that would be her private haven for a while.

A bed with carved pineapple posts centered the room. A goose-down comforter in pale blue with tiny white polka dots suggested cozy nights. There was a fluffy rug for her bare feet, and on the dresser, a pewter vase of blue delphiniums.

Lovely, Katy thought. Who was the decorator? Not that there were any signs of professional decor; everything was comfortably worn. Just enough to invite a person to kick off her shoes and relax, she thought, eyeing the maple rocking chair heaped with plump pillows. A stack of snowy towels and washcloths lay on the trunk at the end of the bed. No private bath?

"No," he said when she voiced her thought. "But it's just down the hall, and you're the only one here." He put down her bags and leaned against the doorsill. "You like it?"

"Yes, I do. Very much." Katy gave a silent gasp as she turned to speak to him. Either the room had shrunk or he'd stepped closer. Of course, neither had happened. As far as she could tell, the room was the same size and he still leaned against the doorsill. She placed her camera on the dresser.

"Do you live here alone, Mr. Logan?"

"Thomas, please. And yes, we're alone. But you needn't worry, I'm quite well known on Orcas Island, and there's a lock on your door." His mouth quirked, and there was a hint of devilry in those heavenly blue eyes. "And I've yet to ravish a female left at my mercy."

Katy found herself blushing again, as much from the melting effect of his azure gaze as from his words. "I was simply trying to get some idea of my surroundings," she replied haughtily. "You mentioned a maid?"

"Uh-huh, Maddie. She comes in at eight and stays until five or so. Your credit card is on record?" he asked without much concern. Katy nodded. "Well, then," he concluded briskly, "I'll leave you to get settled in. Any questions?"

"No, no questions."

His teeth flashed. "I have one. How did you come to choose my place? I don't advertise at all."

"I didn't choose it, my girlfriend did. She lives on the island, so naturally I asked her to find me a decent place to stay," Katy said. He was smiling at her again, his smile especially for her, it suggested. She felt another rush of warmth, this time in the vicinity of her heart.

Disconcerted by her lightning-quick responses to this stranger, she placed a hand on the bedpost to steady her nerves. What's with you today, Katy? she demanded. First his house and now the man!

Realizing he'd asked the name of her friend, Katy hurriedly replied, "Patsy Palmer. Do you know her? She's a potter, has what she calls a 'wee place' at that artists' colony down by the ferry landing."

"Of course I know Patsy. I'll have to remember to thank her," Thomas murmured. Maybe even send her flowers, he thought, listening to Katy's spontaneous little laugh.

He put one of her suitcases on the luggage rack, using the act to cover another quick but thorough study of his guest. Which he'd been doing since that first dazzling glimpse of her, he admitted. Her image was already fairly well set in his mind, the golden curls intent upon escaping from beneath her baseball cap, her apple cheeks and slanting eyebrows, the soft, sweet, generous mouth he had a compelling urge to taste.

His own mouth insisted on curving as he watched her place her pillow on the bed just so. Her eyes were an incredible color, somewhere between purple and blue. Violet, he decided. She was small, even fragile in appearance, but he sensed the steel in that slim spine. Expertly he appraised the white silk blouse tucked into tan slacks, the diamond solitaire that glittered at her throat, the tiny gold watch on her wrist.

Her nails were tapered ovals of soft, glossy pink. Nails that had never dug in a garden, he'd warrant. She wore sandals, and even her toenails were the same shining color as her fingertips. Pedicured feet, he decided. Pretty feet. Not that he had a foot fetish, but... Thomas raked a hand through his hair, a nervous gesture. Not that women made him nervous... Oh, hell. Enough already, he admonished himself.

His guest was beautiful, all right, but he couldn't help wondering at the shadows that haunted those enchanting eyes. What had caused the sadness that lay deep within their depths? Had someone hurt her? A man? Clamping down on his unsettling need to know, Thomas gave himself a brisk mental shake. "As I said, if you need anything... Oh, I'll leave a key on the table by the front door. You can pick it up at your convenience. You can also sign the register later."

"Yes, I will. Thank you."

"You're welcome."

He certainly seemed eager to leave, Katy thought with an unseemly touch of resentment. Biting her bottom lip, she watched him stride out the door. His hair curled at his nape like a little boy's. But this was no little boy, she was quick to warn herself. This was a man, a sinewy length of vibrant masculinity that warmed a woman all over.

He must drive the females on this island crazy, she thought. Patsy, too? Chagrined, Katy turned away to unpack. Even so, she was very much aware of him leaving the room.

It felt a little strange to think she'd be here alone with him. "Oh, Katy, he's the host, for heaven's sake!" she disparaged her nervousness. "Don't go getting any crazy ideas about him."

A late-afternoon breeze wafted through her window, and with it, the sound of Thomas Logan's voice. He was speaking to the cat, chiding it, his laugh gentle.

The same gentleness she had sensed when he'd asked if she was all right. "When you went into orbit just because an airplane flew by a little lower than usual, Kathleen. Idiot!" she muttered.

Realizing she'd called herself an idiot for the third time in less than an hour, Katy smiled at herself. The usually derisive term was actually an affectionate catchword between two sisters. Katy even remembered the first time they'd used it. *Karin, nine years old, red-faced and furious, lobbing Easter eggs at Katy and screeching, "You're an idiot, you know that, Katy? An idiot! I do not like that creepy Bryant Hurst!"*

Punishment was swift, of course; Nell, their beloved nanny, did not tolerate rudeness, not from anyone, and especially not from her young misses...

Oh, Karin, I miss you, I miss you! The lump in Katy's throat, for all its familiarity, was painfully hard to dislodge. Suddenly aching with loneliness and grief, she hugged herself with a little swaying motion until the pain dulled to a manageable level.

With a physical effort, she closed the door on her memories and indulged in an elaborate stretch. Lord, she was tired! Every muscle ached with the strain of her long trip. She glanced at her watch. Six o'clock, too late for a nap and too early for bed. A walk, then, she decided. From her window overlooking the meadow she could see woods and inviting glades. The fragrance of clover and wild grasses beckoned to her.

Katy changed clothes, choosing sneakers, walking shorts and a cotton blouse, then tied the sleeves of a pink cardigan around her shoulders. Her hair, trapped under a baseball hat for so many hours, was a tangled mess and required a thorough brushing. The heavy, loosely curling, perennially tousled mane contained a dozen shades of gold, from dark honey to the palest blond. Leaving it loose around her shoulders, she hurried downstairs.

Thomas Logan was not in sight. She walked through the dining room to the French doors leading out to the back terrace. Borders of pink shrub roses separated the yard from the meadow. A fieldstone path led down the slight incline and impulsively she took it, following the sound of running water.

Just as the name of the B&B suggested, there was indeed a brook and it did tumble over black rocks, through banks of wild yellow iris and tall pink and white foxgloves in full, regal bloom. Beyond, the path ran uphill for a way before forking sharply. She followed the right fork to a gazebo perched near the edge of a bluff that descended almost straight down to the water.

Her absent Mr. Logan was painting the small structure; his lithe torso lengthening as he brought the paintbrush upward in a long, powerful sweep. A sharp little thrill rippled under her skin. Katy stopped, trying to decide whether to go on, or go back.

But, too late; he'd already seen her. "Hello, again," she called, making her way along the stony path. Coming round the side of the gazebo, she gave a little gasp of pleasure.

"Nice view, huh?" he murmured.

"Nice," Katy answered, thinking wryly that *nice* didn't do it justice. Below her, spread out like dark green jewels on a velvet cloth of water, the San Juan Islands lay drowsing in the sunlight. The Washington coast was a dark blur in the distance, and clouds drifted down the highest hills to become tangled in the tops of soaring firs. Her camera was in her room, worse luck. But there would be plenty of time to take pictures.

She looked up and found his gaze on her face. "It's lovely," she said.

"Yeah, lovely." Putting down his brush, he walked over to stand beside her. "I love it. Always have."

"Always? You've lived here all your life, then?"

"No, this was my grandparents' home. I grew up in Baltimore, but I loved to spend the summers here when I was a boy."

She had turned her attention back to the view. While he spoke, Thomas let his gaze play over her again. Honey-toned skin everywhere he looked, face, arms, long shapely legs. Masses of honey-colored hair blowing in the wind.

"I guess you think Tumbling Brook's a pretty fancy name for this place," he said idly.

"I did wonder, yes." She swept out her small hands in a movement that reminded him of butterflies. "It doesn't suit you," she said simply.

"It doesn't, huh?" He chuckled. "Actually, Grandmother named it, and since Grandfather thought she hung the moon, Tumbling Brook it was."

Katy smiled at the colloquial expression. Obviously, his grandfather had adored his grandmother. It must be nice to be adored, she thought with disarming wistfulness.

"Well, the brook does tumble," she said, and they both laughed. "Do you grow the roses? They're lovely."

"Yes, the roses, the flowers, a few choice vegetables. I supply the local merchants with fresh produce." He grinned. "A hobby more than a money-making endeavor."

He was so easy to be with, she reflected. Some small part of her insisted she knew him, from some other time, some other place. A little shaken, Katy reminded herself that he was also a stranger. "Mr. Logan, I need to make a telephone call. Long distance, but I have a calling card. I need to check in with my... family."

"Of course," Thomas said. "Telephone's in the kitchen."

"Thank you." Excusing herself, Katy turned back and followed the left fork for a while. At length, she retraced her steps to the house and called Nell for a brief, reassuring chat.

Hanging up, Katy yawned with catlike languor. Perhaps she'd have that nap, after all.

Katy woke disoriented. Blearily, she noticed the sunset and wondered why Nell had let her sleep through dinner when she was so hungry. Then awareness returned fully and she sat up. This wasn't home and that wasn't her be-

loved nanny-turned-housekeeper she heard stirring downstairs. She sighed. Where was she going to eat tonight? She
hated the thought of getting dressed and going out.

She lay there for a few more minutes, luxuriating in the
perfect warmth of the goose-down comforter. She was still
tired, still drowsy. But if she didn't get up now, she
wouldn't sleep tonight. Well, this was the purpose of her
trip, to rest, relax, unwind. Get away from it all, she reflected, without permitting her mind to explore the *all*.

Her gaze fell upon her camera and the rolls of film she'd
stacked beside it. A freelance writer and photographer, she
had combined her vacation with an assignment from a
travel magazine she had worked with before Karin's death.
At the time Katy had felt ambivalent about accepting it.
Although she had always loved her work, right now it
seemed more of a burden than a pleasure. But both her
therapist and her editor thought it would be good for her.

Well, maybe they were right, she reflected. Maybe
working in this lovely place would revive her zest for life.

Her mind abruptly shifted to the hunger pangs knot-
ting her stomach. They surprised her, for she hadn't really
been hungry for so long she'd almost forgotten how it felt.
It felt pretty good, Katy decided.

Clad only in a tiny gold ankle bracelet, she padded to the
closet in search of a robe. She needed a shower and the
bathroom was down the hall. An inconvenience, but one
often encountered at such establishments.

Catching sight of herself in the full-length mirror on the
closet door, she made a face. Napping had removed some
of her makeup, and mascara darkened the shadows under
her eyes. She wondered what the charming Mr. Logan
would think of her were he to see her right now. Grimacing, she pulled on her robe, opened the bedroom door and
nearly bumped into him.

"Oops! Sorry!" he exclaimed, dropping the towels he'd been holding and catching her arms just below the short, fluttery sleeves of her robe.

His touch on her flesh was electric. Katy jumped from both the unexpected encounter and the lovely sensations racing down her arms. *God, it's been so long since I've had these feelings,* she thought, thoroughly surprised. When she moved, the tips of her breasts touched the hard male chest covered only in a thin T-shirt. She could feel his body heat. And her own.

His quick, indrawn breath gifted her with another shivery thrill.

"Are you okay?" he asked huskily. "I didn't mean to bowl you over."

Strangely reluctant to look at him, she understood why when their eyes met. Something disturbingly strong and splendid flowed between them, something not entirely physical.

"I'm fine, really." Shaken, she pulled away and smoothed her tumbled hair. He knelt to pick up the towels he'd been carrying.

"Oh, I'm glad you have those—I forgot mine," Katy said, somewhat breathlessly.

"I was just bringing these to you. I wasn't sure you had enough. It's been my experience that women require a lot of towels," he drawled.

Experience in what capacity? Holding her tongue, Katy accepted the linens he handed up to her and thanked him.

"You're welcome." As his gaze swept upward, Thomas felt a vital quickening. From his kneeling position he had a fine view of sleek, satin-covered thighs and the sweet flare of her hips. Seen from below, her breasts were high and pointed. *Proud breasts,* he thought, *small, but rich enough to satisfy the sudden itch in his hands.*

He stood up and smiled at her. Her lips parted and he watched them curve up at the corners in a little answering smile that was at once seductive and innocent of seduction. How would her mouth taste? he wondered. And how long had it been since he had been so acutely aware of a woman?

She stepped around him, the shimmery robe clinging to her enticing form. She smelled delicious, he thought distractedly. Why did she want to shower?

As she walked from him, desire coiled low in his stomach, a deluge of yearning that stunned him a little, for it was mixed with other things. Nameless things, but very much there.

When she glanced over her shoulder, his tight mouth softened. Her face had the fresh, fragile beauty of a wildflower.

"Just a minute, Katy," he said abruptly. "There are a few other things I want to tell you. One is that the living room is for your pleasure, also the kitchen should you want to prepare tea or coffee. There's television downstairs... Let's see, what else? The front door isn't locked until eleven. After that, you'll need your key. Oh, one more thing—what are you doing for dinner tonight?"

Unprepared for his question, she stammered, "Why, I— I'd planned to go out for dinner, that is, if you'd kindly point me toward a restaurant," she ended with a small laugh. "Do you have a map of the island?"

"Yes. But I thought, well, you've obviously had a full day already, so if you'd like, you can have a bite with me tonight."

Her mouth shaped an "Oh!" before she said, "But feeding your guests dinner isn't one of your services, is it?"

Such beautiful eyes, Thomas thought. Big and dark and vulnerable. His voice gentled. "Not ordinarily. But now and then I do go out of my way for a guest. Dinner's nothing fancy, just ham and fresh pinto beans and corn bread. Raspberry shortcake for dessert, though," he added

as an inducement when he saw doubt clouding her face.
"I'd be delighted to have you join me."

Katy bit her lip, devilishly tempted despite her habitual
wariness. It would feel so good just to put on a comfortable outfit and have dinner here, rather than driving to a
restaurant. Down strange roads, she reminded herself. And
it would be nighttime when she returned.

Better to keep your distance, Katy. "Thank you, but
I've had a nap and now I feel a need to get out for a
while." Her smile was spontaneous, warm. "But I appreciate your kind offer."

"Anytime," he said, apparently unbothered by her rejection.

He didn't move. She hurried into the bathroom, closed
the door behind her and leaned against its heavy surface.
She could feel his presence tugging at her even through the
wood.

After a moment she straightened. She'd forgotten her
shampoo. Opening the door, she peeked out. He was going down the stairs. She hurried to her bedroom, then
stopped just outside the door as she noticed for the first
time the photographic gallery he had created on the hallway walls.

More family pictures: babies, graduations, weddings,
outings, all the special occasions that bond a group of
people. But what riveted her attention were two pictures of
Thomas Logan.

In one, he waved from the cockpit window of a plane
that bore the insignia T. L. Airlines and a decal of Pega-
sus, the mythical winged horse. In the second picture, he
stood beside a sleek little jet that flaunted the same proud
insignia. He wore a captain's hat and a uniform bearing
that unmistakable logo.

Katy recoiled. So this was his true profession, she
thought with chilling disappointment. He was a pilot.

Becoming conscious of her tense stance, Katy released her breath and drew in air. This is absurd, she told herself. Why should you care what he does for a living?

But a *pilot!* She shivered and hurried into her room.

A moment later she returned to the bathroom. As she closed the door, she heard him downstairs, laughing as he scolded the cat. The sound of that husky laughter struck some vibrant chord deep inside her. Bemused by her spontaneous reaction, she grasped a corner of the mirrored shower stall to steady herself.

His effect upon her was startling, to say the least, Katy thought flippantly, trying to minimize its intensity. But she had never felt such a warm and immediate response to a man. And she knew with a profound feminine awareness that the feeling had been mutual. This thrilled her, and confused her. If she wanted intimacy, there was nothing stopping her. In fact, a little summer fling could be an exciting new experience.

"All you have to do is whistle," Katy murmured with a wry smile for her rosy-cheeked image. She already knew he could whistle...

She sobered, her features tightening as she came back down to earth with a jarring thud. What if it didn't remain just a pleasant little fling?

He's a pilot, she reminded herself, and shuddered as a host of images shot through her mind with the swiftness, and destruction, of summer lightning. To Katy, the plane he touched so proudly was a symbol of devastating loss. Flying was synonymous with death.

Hot tears surged to her eyes, then spilled down her cheeks. All day she had tried not to think of the date. An anniversary of sorts, she thought bleakly. The nine-month anniversary of the death of the person she loved more than she loved herself, her sister Karin.

Karin, her identical twin, her other self. Katy drew a breath against the stabbing hurt. Love, to her, had become simply another word for loss. Fate had taken her entire family, parents, grandparents, sister. She'd even lost the man—had been *dumped* by the man, she corrected with searing honesty—she had loved. Or thought she had loved. Whatever it was, it didn't matter, she decided, suddenly ragingly furious. Love, lust, illusion. Whatever you called it, it was still devastatingly painful when it ended.

So she'd become wary. "Built myself a wall against love," Katy conceded wearily. But wariness was both natural and sensible, she insisted as Thomas Logan's clear blue gaze shot to mind. She was still in mourning. And she was still healing from the destruction of the hopes and dreams she'd brought into her marriage.

She'd had far too much trauma in her life already. No more risks equaled no more pain. An intelligent rationale, Katy told herself fiercely, swiping at tears.

Suddenly, she wished she had someone to hold her. But as usual, the only arms around her were her own.

Two

Thomas Logan walked downstairs still smarting from his encounter with the elusive Miss Lawrence. He wasn't accustomed to having his dinner invitations rejected.

Besides, it made no sense for her to go out to eat when she was obviously exhausted. A nap hadn't done that much for her, he thought moodily.

A fine rain had begun falling, shortening the dusky evening into twilight. His mood lowered even more. He didn't mind eating alone, didn't even think about it, most times. But he would have enjoyed looking across the table at that intriguing face tonight. Enjoyed it tremendously, in fact. And they could have talked, answered the dozens of questions whirling in his mind. He wanted to know everything about her.

"Curious, the feelings she stirs up," he thought aloud. Sighing, he went to the kitchen and checked the fragrant pot of beans he'd been cooking. There was no better eating than fresh pinto beans, in his opinion. He grinned at himself. This from a man who used to dine in New York's trendiest restaurants?

Just then, the telephone rang; someone wanted a reservation for the weekend. For a moment he nearly refused. Then common sense asserted itself. He'd hate to have to explain to his mother why he couldn't provide a room to her best friends, especially when he had rooms to spare. The house was big, four bedrooms and two baths upstairs, the master suite and living areas downstairs.

After jotting down expected arrival times and replacing the receiver, he took the pan of corn bread from the oven and set it on a cooling rack. Bending over sent a dull ache down one hip, a rainy-day reminder of injuries sustained in the car wreck that had nearly killed him.

His thoughts lingered on the subject. Before his near-death experience, he'd been a Wall Street wizard whose main interest in life was what he'd arrogantly termed the easy-money game. Making money was a power-trip that had utterly consumed him, until the day he'd rounded a curve too fast and sent his Porsche and himself over the edge of a deep ravine.

During the ensuing days of pain and confusion, he realized what a joke his life had been up to that point. Motivated by the radical change in his outlook, he'd left New York and returned to the islands to help his adored grandparents run this lovely inn.

Remembering, he shook his head in wry amusement. No one could believe that he'd given up his glamorous, high-profile life-style for the rough urbanity of Orcas Island. They'd believe even less how happy he was here, he thought, uncapping a beer. He had taken up flying immediately upon settling here, got his license, discovered the sheer, rapturous glory of soaring into the sky. He could, and often did, spend hours in his plane, alone or taking people out on chartered flights.

True, since his grandparents had moved to Florida, it was lonely here sometimes, on nights like this, especially. But for the most part he was content. Or would be, if the rest of his needs were met, he conceded with another sigh. He was thirty-five, time to be getting on with the rest of his life. But he hadn't found anyone he wanted to get on *with*, he mused as he uncovered the baked ham.

He had many women friends because he was a friendly, caring man. But they just stayed friends. Still, some were eminently qualified to become Mrs. Thomas Miles Logan. But all or nothing was his motto, though sometimes he wondered if such a thing as deep, passionate love really existed. Certainly passion did, and love, too. But together?

And if it did exist, would he ever find it?

A sound from upstairs tightened his stomach. Katy. A pretty name. A pretty lady. Who had no business going out tonight.

He fetched a tray and set it with silverware, dipped beans into a bowl, sliced the savory ham and cut a wedge of golden corn bread. Angel food cake layered with fresh raspberries and whipped cream made a sumptuous dessert, at least in his opinion. Then he spared a thought as to why he was bringing her a tray of food. The gesture probably came from having three sisters, he decided. His mother's words rolled across his mind: "Watch out for your sisters, Thomas. Take care of your sisters, Thomas."

Chuckling at the cozy memory, he carried the tray upstairs and tapped on Katy's door.

She opened it, her damp hair drifting around her shoulders as she stared up at him. She was wrapped in a long white terry-cloth robe that clung to every gorgeous inch of her. Any brotherly thoughts instantly vanished from Thomas's mind.

"Good evening."

"Good evening. Oh!" Katy's eyes flew wide as she noticed the tray.

"I saw no sense in your going out tonight just to get something to eat," he said gruffly. "So I fixed you a tray."

"Well!" She looked at the tray and then up at him again. "My goodness, you shouldn't have done that. I mean, it's really very kind of you, but totally unnecessary. Oh, Lord, that does smell good!" She sighed, inhaling the savory aromas.

Thomas gave her a smug smile. He was a damn fine cook, if he did say so himself. "Tastes as good as it smells. Now you can stay in and get a good night's sleep, instead of wandering around the island in the dark."

Her eyes narrowed, instantly challenging his sensible suggestion. All right, *command,* but still sensible, Thomas insisted, holding out the tray.

"I'm sure the food is delicious," she said, taking the tray. "I may still go out, however."

"It's raining and the roads are narrow two-lanes, with few street signs," he said, frowning.

"I think I can find my way around. After all, I do live in a large city," she returned with a hint of coolness that irked the devil out of him.

"Well, whatever you choose to do, enjoy the meal," Thomas said. He turned on his heel and strode back downstairs.

"Mr. Logan?" Her soft voice stopped him on the landing.

"Yes?"

"Thank you."

He heard her door close. "You're welcome," he mumbled, feeling pushed and pulled by the change in that silken voice.

The telephone was ringing again. No more guests, he thought irritably. But it was the airport. He had an eleven o'clock charter in the morning.

Thomas jotted down the client's name, then just stood
there, staring, unseeing, out the kitchen window. His mind
had already winged back to the woman upstairs. He'd seen
those violet eyes flash, seen the twist of mouth that be-
spoke fire and temper. She looked as cool as a glass of ice
water, but that mouth would never kiss a man coolly. She'd
put her entire self into every hot, passionate kiss, scatter a
man's senses to the wind, wrap his heart around those
slender fingers...

With a snort of self-disgust, Thomas hauled himself
back to reality. What the hell was he thinking? This
morning he didn't even know she existed, and here he
stood dithering about kisses and passion and wrapped-up
hearts.

"It's been too long, Logan," he muttered. Maybe he
ought to clean the kitchen. At least put the food away. But
he didn't feel like cleaning kitchens. What he felt like
was...

Making another sound of disgust, he decided to sit on
the porch a while and let the cool evening air chill the many
little fevers inside him.

Katy jerked awake with a soft cry. She had been dream-
ing, that recurring nightmare that tormented her sleep. She
exhaled a long, tremulous breath. Thank goodness it
wasn't one of her really bad dreams. Sometimes she awoke
screaming.

Sitting up, she drew the drapes and peered out at the new
day. It was only four-thirty, but daylight, soft and misty,
streamed in through the windows. The air had a tang to it
that was almost a taste on her tongue.

She stretched, yawning, and touched her eyelids. They
didn't feel red or swollen, or even gritty. She hadn't cried
anymore last night. She hadn't gone out, either, just enjoyed her delicious meal and went to bed to read a paperback romance. They were her weakness, tales of beautiful

love and dreams and happy-ever-afters. She wasn't sure any of it was true, but some secret part of herself wanted to believe it was possible.

Unbidden, her thoughts leaped to the memory of Thomas's blue eyes glinting at her when she had opposed his will. Preposterous, of course. Who was Thomas Logan to decide if she should or should not go out?

Thomas. She liked his name, the soft, clipped sound of it. He was certainly full of himself, she reflected, swinging her feet to the floor. And so good to look at that just picturing his face pleased every part of her lissome body.

Reminding herself that California was full of good-looking men, Katy tumbled out of bed and headed for the bathroom.

To her annoyance, she brought a nagging sense of guilt with her. Bossy or not, Thomas had been nice to her last night and she'd been a bit, well, ungracious.

"Not too smart, Katy," she muttered, slathering cleanser on her face. "After all, you're spending several weeks with the man as host, you can at least be friendly."

Friendly, yes, but that's all, she warned herself, rinsing off the cream. If you can't think of him as just your host, consider the man an intriguing new acquaintance.

Satisfied with her pragmatic solution, she dried her face and patted on an oatmeal mask. Then she walked back to her room, snuggled under the comforter once more and finished her book.

At six o'clock she stepped into the hallway again and listened for a moment. Noises from the kitchen, and then the aroma of hot coffee wafted up the stairs, a siren song she couldn't resist.

After a quick shower, she dressed in jeans and a yellow linen shirt, and swirled her hair atop her head. Contrarily, the open window drew her and she scampered onto the window seat. The sunlight was stronger now, and shadows pooled under tall fir trees. A streak of blue caught her eye as a tiny bird landed on the lawn and began a diligent search for insects.

Splendor in the grass, Katy thought with humor. Suddenly eager, for the first time in months, to experience whatever the day would bring, she ran downstairs to the kitchen.

Except for the calico cat sleeping on the windowsill, the house appeared to be empty. She glanced at the table, set with a pink cloth and white china. Coffee steamed in a pot. Pecan muffins rested on the sideboard. The fragrance of bacon made her mouth water. Where was he?

Outside, she bet, enjoying the glorious morning. And here he came, strolling through the yard carrying a basket of freshly picked strawberries. A fragile sense of well-being stole over her. Katy let out her breath, unaware that she'd been holding it, as he walked in and let the screen door slam behind him.

Seeing her, he stopped, eyes crinkling, a smile tugging at his fine mouth as he looked over her formfitting attire.

Their greetings collided. Deciding she had some fence-mending to do, Katy laughed and said, "Those strawberries look wonderful. I don't know when I've last had them right from the patch. Mr. Logan—"

"Thomas, please."

"Thomas. I want to thank you again for the tray last night. It truly was a godsend, I didn't really feel like going out," she confessed. "I realize I may have been a little ungracious about that." She paused, shifting under his keen gaze.

"Why was that?" He motioned her to sit down at the table.

Obliging him, she replied, "I suppose it's because I don't enjoy being ordered around. You were just a trifle bossy, Mr.... Thomas." Why was it so hard to say his name? Because it implied an intimacy she didn't want? And *did* want?

"Sorry about that," he said, looking not in the least sorry about that. "Force of habit, I suppose."

"Oh? Your women like to be bossed around, do they?" she asked, then could have bitten her tongue.

"Sometimes." He grinned at the berries he began rinsing. "When it's by me."

She nibbled back a smile—he was impossible!

Unfolding her napkin, she inquired, "Am I your only guest?"

"Thus far. An older couple are coming in this weekend. Friends of my folks, so I couldn't say no."

"Oh." Intrigued, she asked, "Did you want to say no?"

Apparently her question caught him by surprise; Thomas glanced at her, then slowly shook his head as if perplexed.

"I suppose guests can be a bother at times," she mused.

"At times." His quick glance was accompanied by a grin this time. "Present company excepted. Help yourself." Dumping the berries into a ceramic colander, he set it on a plate then on the table. "I'll just reheat these muffins and we can eat. Did you sleep well?"

"Very well, thank you. That goose-down comforter is marvelous. And I love that old-fashioned fan. In fact, I love your house. Ah." She sighed as he took the muffins from the microwave and emptied them into a cloth-lined basket. Everything he did was done with an expert's ease. Glancing at the tall figure in navy blue slacks and shirt, she commented, "You seem to be an old hand at this."

"Oh, I've cooked for myself for years. Even before I took up the bachelor's life in the Big Apple, in fact." Bringing the coffeepot with him, he sat down beside her.

"You lived in New York?"

He cocked an eyebrow. "Why are you so surprised at that?"

"Oh! Well, from Baltimore to a rustic little island is a big stretch, not to mention New York City." Katy fought a brief and unsuccessful battle with her curiosity. "Were you a pilot before you moved here? I noticed the hallway pictures," she hurriedly explained. "T. L. Airlines. Yours?"

Thomas nodded. "Mine. And yes, I flew planes before, but just for pleasure. When I decided to make this my permanent home, I needed something to keep me busy. There was already a small charter service on the island, so I bought it, added two more planes and voila! T. L. Airlines: offering commuter service between San Juan Islands and SEA-TAC as well as private charters."

She smiled, touched by the pride in his voice. "How many planes do you have?"

"Five in all."

"And you run this B&B, too? My, you are a busy man!" She tasted her coffee. "Umm, good coffee. You said your grandparents owned the house. Have they passed on?" she asked with exquisite delicacy.

"Heck, no! They just *moved* on. To Florida, where it's warm and sunny all year round. I was fed up with New York and they were tired of rain and cold, so I bought this place from them, and they flew off like two lovebirds escaped from their cage!"

Katy laughed delightedly, her spirits lifting as her laughter ignited his. Something warm and sparkling had entered the atmosphere. Her heart, her body, even her soul responded to its effervescent magic.

"You really like this house, hmm?" he said.

Her eyes veiled. "Yes."

"Me, too." Sensing her unease, Thomas swallowed his probing questions and cast about for something that would bring them close again. "You ever lived on a farm?"

She laughed. "Certainly I have. A whole summer, in fact. I loved it."

"You're kidding!" He squinted at her. "A working farm?"

"Yes. I milked cows, baled hay, fed pigs, drove a tractor, you name it." She took a bite of buttered muffin. "Mmm, this is good. The butter, too."

"The butter is made by the nuns on the next island. They have the smallest dairy in the world, three cows. They also make cheese."

Somewhat bemused, he stared at her. Unbelievable that those elegant hands had ever milked a cow. And baled hay? She must not be as fragile as she looked.

He ate a handful of strawberries while he examined her heart-shaped face. Her wide, generous mouth was a delicious contrast to the aristocratic little nose. Her hair was tamed today, firmly caught in a knot that was already spilling curls down her neck. Silver earrings graced her ears, and a wide, matching bracelet clamped one thin wrist.

Why was she so thin? Because that was the style now, all skin and bones and sharp angles. Although she didn't look to have too many sharp angles. None at all, in fact.

He put another muffin and two strips of bacon on her plate. "You a vegetarian?" he asked.

"Not entirely. Not with bacon this good. Organic?"

"Yeah, friend-grown pork. No chemicals, no growth hormones. I sure wouldn't have figured you for the farm life. What are you doing in California?"

"I'm a writer and photographer—travel books, scenic tours, that sort of thing, for magazines."

Without thinking, she poured him a cup of coffee and took pleasure in the small service.

It pleased him, too, inordinately. He shook his dark head. "Fascinating. But I'd have guessed you for an actress."

Her nose wrinkled. "Hardly."

"How'd you get started in photography?"

"Just came naturally, I guess. I loved taking pictures even as a girl. I had one of those cheap little cameras that took fuzzy pictures, but I thought they were great.'' Katy stirred her coffee round and round as the past crowded in with surprising force. ''You're lucky to have such a close relationship with your grandparents,'' she said softly.

''You don't?'' Thomas watched her spoon make another lap around the cup before she answered.

''No. Dad married Mother against his parents' wishes. So there was very little communication between them. It's ironic, really,'' she said musingly. ''That they inherited us, I mean. After our parents died, we lived with Grammy Rose, Mom's mother, for three years. A lovely, loving woman... Then she died, and we were passed on to our paternal grandparents in Boston. None of us were very happy about the situation.''

Katy halted, chagrined at her loose tongue. ''I'm sorry, I didn't mean for this to get so personal.''

''No! Don't be sorry,'' Thomas protested. He was aware of her discomfort, but his need to know the forces that had molded and shaped this beguiling woman had become incredibly strong. ''Why weren't you happy?'' he asked urgently. ''How old were you?''

''Seven.'' Her voice thinned. ''Our grandparents were...well, they were old. Even though they were only in their sixties, they were old, quite incapable of reorganizing their life-style around two little girls.''

''I see.'' Suddenly, nebulously angry, Thomas hunched over his coffee mug. ''What was their solution?''

''Boarding schools. The very best, of course. But we did spend the holidays at home.''

''That must have been tough,'' he said, and for an instant she thought he had touched her, so warm and soft was his voice.

Tensing, she sipped her coffee and welcomed its scalding heat on her tongue. To her astonishment, she was battling an urge to pour out her entire life story.

She shrugged. "Not so tough. We had everything we needed."

Except love, Thomas thought grimly. But instinct warned him against displaying his compassion. She might mistake it for pity. "You said two little girls," he remembered. "Who was the other one?"

"Karin. My twin sister."

"Good heavens, you mean there are two of you?" he asked with mock horror.

"No, not anymore."

Thomas sobered. Her lashes swept down, but not before he caught a glimpse of the sadness sheening those darkened eyes. His voice roughened. "What happened?"

"She died last year."

The starkness of her reply unsettled Katy as much as Thomas. Why on earth had she told him about Karin? It was too personal, too intimate! She shot to her feet with a glance at her watch.

"Gosh, look at the time! I've got to go—I'm meeting Patsy in a few minutes. She's showing me some of the sights. Breakfast was wonderful, Thomas. Thank you."

Thomas gave a courteous but absentminded response. He was thinking how much *he'd* like to show her the island. "Will you be home late?"

Her eyes narrowed.

Back off, Logan, Thomas castigated himself. *She's a paying guest. It's none of your business when she comes in!*

But he damn well wanted to make it his business.

"Well, that really doesn't matter," he went on briskly. "You have a key, so... Enjoy your day, Katy."

"You, too," she said, and then she was gone, leaving behind a strange new emptiness.

Katy found her way back to the harbor, and soon located her friend's house and store. Patsy rushed out shrieking with delight at seeing her again. Although they kept in touch, it had been four years since Patsy left California. The women were college friends. A friendship that had lasted through thick and thin, Katy thought, hugging Patsy with the same wild fervor.

"How do you like the B&B I recommended?" Patsy asked as they started toward the house.

"It's lovely, of course."

"Oh, good." Patsy gave her a sly glance. "And the host?"

"He's lovely, too," Katy said dryly. "It's really odd that you forgot to mention him."

"Um, well, you know. What do you think of him?"

"He seems nice enough," Katy allowed. "Bossy, though."

"Yeah, he is that. Comes from all those women chasing him around the islands," Patsy said, nodding agreement with herself.

"Does that include you?"

"No. For some obscure reason, there's never been any chemistry between that gorgeous thing and me. My hormones must be getting thin." An eyebrow arched. "How are yours doing?"

"The last time I checked, my hormones were doing just fine. Are we going to stand here on the steps or can we go inside?"

Laughing, Patsy ushered her through the door. The house was small, just two rooms and a bath. One room to sleep, eat and cook in, the other to display her pottery wares and store supplies.

"This is why I didn't invite you to stay with me," she said. "I wanted to, believe me, but as you can see, we just don't have any room."

"We?"

"Yeah, we. Right now I've got a roommate. His name is Ken. That's his picture on the mantel."

Sighing, Patsy pushed at the lock of red hair falling across her face. She was freckled all over, and beautiful, Katy thought.

"He's quite a hunk, Patsy," she said as she studied the picture. "Is it serious?"

"Not yet. This is sort of a tryout period." Patsy's little nose wrinkled. "I mean, hey, you road test a new car, don't you? Why not a new relationship? Might keep a person from making another mistake. Which, in my case, would make me a three-time loser," she said with acerbic humor. Eyes bright, she cocked her head. "You, though, hold the record for short-lived marital harmony. I mean, really, Katy, nine months? What kind of a marriage was it, for heaven's sake?"

"A bad one. He was a womanizer and control freak." Katy's mouth twisted wryly. "Sort of like that soap-opera role he's playing now." Using her bitter drollery as armor against remembered pain, she sketched a picture of the marriage she had ended five years ago. "Everyone seemed to know what kind of guy he was but me. Well, me and Karin, I should say. Even she was fooled by his charm. But he *was* an actor, and so handsome, so boyishly sweet—I was nuts about the man, even thought he was just being masterful when he insisted on supervising my every move."

She gave a dry laugh. "But then, everyone loved Rhys! And Rhys loved everyone. At least he tried to. When I had the effrontery to object to his infidelities, he walked out.

"Anyway," she concluded crisply, "I'm not keen to try it again, with tor without a road test."

Dismissing the subject, Katy picked up one of the pottery pieces strewn around the room, a tall jug done in cream, rust, gold and brown, with an uneven band of blue. The colors formed a pattern that resembled an otherworldly landscape. "This is lovely, Patsy. You've really improved since you left California."

"It's island living. The serenity just sort of seeps into my hands when they're on the wheel, and voilà!, I get a piece like that." Patsy hesitated, then asked softly, "Katy? You still having problems? I mean, well, are you still scared of planes and flying?"

"Petrified," Katy said simply. "Every time I remember that plane crash, I—I just can't get past it, Patsy. Seeing it was so close to *living* it! I felt everything, everything!" She stopped and drew a shuddery breath. "I'm sorry, I didn't mean to get so emotional. Look, I know we haven't discussed Karin yet and I know she's heavy on your mind. But I didn't come here to cry on your shoulder, honey. I'm here to laugh and have fun. To forget, for a little while, anyway. Let's just enjoy being together again. So, are you ready to show me the town?"

"That won't take long," Patsy said. "Eastsound is ten by fifteen. Blocks, that is. But there are lots of little shops, and the town itself is picturesque, especially this time of year with flowers blooming all over the place. Do you still like yellow roses? There are some gorgeous ones at Putte's Café."

"I adore yellow roses," Katy declared. The two women shared another hug, then went out to Patsy's Jeep for their sight-seeing tour.

On the way to town, they stopped at an overlook, and Katy got out with her camera in hand. "Step into the picture, Pat," she wheedled. Patsy, red hair blowing in the wind, knee-deep in wildflowers and lush green grass, was a gorgeous advertisement for the island.

A short while later, as they wandered through the small town, Katy snapped pictures in seemingly haphazard sequence. This was the first assignment she had accepted since her sister's death and she was grateful that she still possessed a keen eye for detail. Although she wasn't an artist, she did enjoy creating the pictorial equivalent of a painting. She and Karin had planned to open a gallery that would feature mainly photographic art . . .

"It's nearly noon." Patsy shattered her pensive reverie. "Let's go have lunch and I'll tell you all about my sweetie."

"Super!" Katy said, shoving back the painful memory. "I'm starving!"

Dusk had long since fallen when the car pulled into his driveway. Thomas had been listening for it and his immense relief irritated him. He hadn't been able to get Katy out of his mind all day. He knew it was crazy to be so preoccupied with a woman he'd just met, crazy to be listening for her footsteps on the porch.

Nevertheless, anticipation danced in his blood. And just what are you anticipating, Logan? he mocked. He checked his watch again. Almost ten o'clock. She'd had another long day.

He stepped forward as she came into the house. They both stopped abruptly. An awkwardness hung between them that neither fully understood. All Thomas knew was that he was very glad to see her and the gladness tightened his throat unmercifully.

"Hello," she said, putting a hand on the newel post as if to show him she meant to go right upstairs.

"Hi. How are you?"

"Fine. And you?"

"Fine. I'm fine. Never better," he said.

He began laughing, leaving her torn between annoyance and amusement. "You weren't waiting up for me, were you?" she asked, tilting her head to look up at him.

"No, I was just reading. I heard you come in so I thought I'd check and make sure you were okay. I mean, it *is* late."

"Yes, it is," she agreed coolly.

"Very late." Thomas scowled, his self-irritation growing. Why was he acting like this? He'd never bothered worrying about any of his other guests. His sisters again, no doubt. Reining in his sudden wild urge to hug her, he went on with exaggerated dignity, "I'm overstepping again, so sue me. I was simply concerned that you might have difficulty finding your way here after dark. The roads are rather badly marked."

Katy was trying to be gracious, but his *concern* acted like a lash on sensitive skin. Damned if she would account for her time away from this house! She'd had enough of that from her husband. He had needed to control her every action...

But this was Thomas, Katy thought, jerking herself back to the present. And he did have a point. "I'm sorry, Thomas, I do appreciate your concern." She sighed. Why did she feel she had just yielded something with her soft apology? "Actually, I did take a couple of wrong turns. But I'm here now. I wonder, would you have any of those raspberries left? The ones you were bringing in yesterday when I arrived."

Was it only yesterday? she thought with a small shock. It seemed much longer. "I didn't have dessert tonight and I'd like some to nibble on in my room."

"There are a few left." Turning, he led the way to the kitchen.

Katy stopped beside him as he opened the refrigerator and suddenly found herself caught between him and the counter. Her nerves jumped as their eyes met. She felt too warm. Warmth quickly turned to heat. His gaze fell to her lips. He shifted, closer somehow and her heart was pounding.

He didn't touch her, but he might as well have. The sensation was there, on her skin, in the palms of his hands.

He didn't kiss her, but he could taste the kiss, imagine mouth meeting mouth, body meeting body.

Hard to soft, masculinity to femininity. Desire licked at his skin like little tongues of flame.

His eyes deepened, intense and hot.

She wondered if hers were dark with the smoke of her own desire. If they were, she couldn't help it.

She was angry. Angry at him for being so attractive. Angry at herself for being so drawn to him. She refused to shrink back against the counter. Instead, she stood her ground, meeting his gaze steadily, defiantly.

It was the defiance that got to Thomas. She looked as crushable as an eggshell, yet that pointed chin was stuck firmly in the air. A sneaky little worm of shame curled in his gut. *Logan, you ass, you must have the worst case of lust in the whole damn world.*

Expelling a long breath, he shifted his gaze, took out the berries and shut the refrigerator door. At least he'd put a name to what ailed him. That always made a man feel better. He stepped away from her and reached for a smaller bowl.

"I nearly kissed you," he said matter-of-factly.

She cleared her throat. "I know."

"What would you have done if I had?"

"Stopped you."

His eyes challenged. "Would you?"

"Yes." Katy leaned against the counter and regarded him with quick, sparkling mischief. "Going a few rounds with the island's resident Lothario isn't on my agenda to-night."

Amusement tugged at his mouth. "Now who have you been talking to?" he chided, eyes twinkling. "Patsy? I swear, that woman's convinced I have a regular harem stashed on the island."

She arched an eyebrow. "And you don't?"

"No, I believe in quality not quantity," Thomas retorted with an easy shrug. "Your raspberries, ma'am." He swept a hand toward the table. "Here, sit down here and

eat them," he invited like the gentleman he was most of the
time.

Becoming aware of the warm, easy intimacy that had
crept between them, Katy felt a stab of alarm. "Thank
you, but I'm about all talked out after spending the day
with Patsy," she confided. "If you don't mind, I'd like to
eat them in my room."

"Sure." He handed her the small bowl of berries.

She took them, her smile suddenly shy. "Thanks again,
Thomas, for the berries, and for caring. I really am grateful, even if—" her nose wrinkled "—I don't act like it
sometimes. I just don't like answering to anyone, I guess.
Well, good night."

"Good night, Katy," he said huskily.

Controlling her urge to flee from those discerning blue
eyes, Katy strolled to the staircase, and ascended the car-
peted risers with slightly more speed.

She wanted to shrug it off. All of it, him, the kiss she'd
craved despite her denial, the excitement still rocketing
through her bloodstream.

The tender yearning in her heart.

"Impossible!" she whispered.

She wondered if he had flown today. *Just imagining him
up there, his beautiful body entrusted to the fragile fabric
of a plane, his very life at risk...* She shuddered, her mind
caught and held in memory's harsh grasp.

Gradually, the evening's drowsy silence stole around her
like a soft cashmere cloak. Katy sat down on the window
seat and closed her eyes, marveling at the complexity of
her feelings. Before coming here—or before meeting
Thomas Logan, she amended—she could pinpoint her
emotions with deadly accuracy.

Right now they were as wildly tangled as a cat's ball of
yarn.

Three

For the second morning in a row, Katy was up early to have breakfast with Patsy. She showered and dressed with equal haste. Slinging a tote over her shoulder, she ran downstairs. But this time, unlike yesterday, the sound of her footsteps brought Thomas from the kitchen.

"Katy, wait a minute," he said, and caught her arm.

Her skin felt the heat of his fingers. Just his touch set her heart beating faster. For an instant, Katy felt outraged; she simply wasn't used to reacting this strongly to a man, and why didn't he stop it, whatever *it* was!

Her mouth quirked with quick self-humor. "Good morning to you, too, Thomas."

He laughed. "Good morning, Katy."

The excitement his nearness created made her breath catch. Realizing how much she liked this man was another hindrance to normal breathing. Well, she'd liked her ex-husband, too, at first, Katy reminded herself. A gifted actor as well as an exciting, charismatic hunk whose bedroom eyes promised heaven on earth for the right woman, Rhys had played his role well, the tender, caring quintessential male. But she'd soon found out that what she liked went no deeper than the beguiling twist of facial muscles that passed for his smile.

She'd been a fool, Katy freely admitted. But even a fool could learn the dangers of accepting someone at face value.

Her reflective moment had a restorative effect. Putting a hand on the doorknob, she smiled and said, "You'll have to excuse me, I'm in kind of a rush this morning."

"Not even time for breakfast?"

"'Fraid not," she said lightly.

The curve of his mouth melted something.

"Okay, how about meeting me in town for lunch?"

"That sounds lovely," Katy said with an involuntary little sigh. *It does but you can't,* she told herself sternly. *You've already accepted Patsy's luncheon invitation, and to cancel out on a girlfriend for a man is the height of rudeness.* "But I've already made other plans."

He didn't reply. Katy raised her gaze to the blueness of his and felt her knees weaken. A swirl of resentment steadied her. Rhys had been a master at weakening feminine limbs, she reminded herself with pragmatic irony. Thomas was still holding her arm. Pointedly, she looked down at his hand.

He released her, his eyes flinting. "I see. Well, then, as they say, have a nice day, Katy."

She hesitated, knowing he'd taken it wrong. After a moment, she touched his hand. "You, too, Thomas." Flashing him a quick smile, she hurried across the porch and down the walk to her car.

Strange how often she thought of her ex-husband lately. Usually when Thomas got too close, she realized. Well, you use the only yardstick you have to measure by.

Unfortunately, her pragmatic conclusion had little impact on the confusion that filtered through her mind like drifts of fog. By the time she reached Patsy's house, her mood was flat.

The lively redhead's good spirits were infectious and soon had Katy laughing again. They sat at the dinette in its corner nook, eating fresh croissants made at a local bakery. Feeling at ease with her warmhearted friend, Katy talked freely of her life, her career and her hopes for the future. With more difficulty, she spoke of the beautiful condominium she and Karin had shared.

"I'm putting it on the market when I return. Nell agrees with me. It's too big for just the two of us. And too, there are so many reminders of Karin in that place." She forced a smile as Patsy touched her hand in quick compassion. "But surely the worst part is over by now," Katy said. "Except for these dreams. They still come, sometimes they're relatively mild, sometimes they're just dreadful."

Patsy's inviting gaze compelled her to continue, and they talked the morning away, their conversation interrupted only by the occasional tourist coming to the shop to buy a piece of pottery.

Belatedly, Patsy remembered their plans for the day. "First we'll go down to the kiln and pick up some vases I left to be fired. Then we'll meet Ken for lunch at his restaurant. After that, you and I are going sight-seeing with your work in mind."

Nightlife hereabouts left something to be desired, Katy learned on the drive. Ken had recently opened a restaurant-club, a risky business since the islands were not for the party crowd. "We're all laid-back and relaxed around here," Patsy said.

"I noticed. With Thomas, I mean. He seems very easygoing."

"He is now. You should have seen him when he first came to live here. Nerves all tied up in knots... But he's mellowed out beautifully. So have I. Maybe you ought to give yourself a few months here, Katy. Maybe you wouldn't be so fabulously thin.'' Patsy heaved a sigh. ''Every time I try to diet, all I can think about is what I'll eat next.''

Katy just laughed. Patsy had a splendid figure.

So did Ken, she observed later at lunch. He was tall and muscular, with a bit of swagger in his walk, she noticed. Patsy obviously adored him, and even Katy couldn't help liking such a charming, personable man.

But it was hard to discern his deeper feelings for Patsy. Katy hoped with all her heart that her friend's love was reciprocated.

The club wasn't much, just an old building spruced up with some paint and polish. It was comfortable, though, and the food was very good. She sincerely wished Ken luck on his endeavor.

Afterward, she and Patsy loaded her cameras and spent the rest of the day sight-seeing. Patsy was an exuberant guide and they shot several rolls of film. But the light wasn't particularly good, and Katy doubted she had anything worthwhile for their efforts.

At around four, she returned to the inn to bathe and change for dinner. Thomas wasn't in sight and she felt disappointed when she left to have dinner with Patsy and Ken.

After dining on some very good fish from local waters, they sat in the club a while.

While chatting with her companions, Katy suddenly realized she didn't know what day it was. Time was seamless here. But it was Thursday. She had arrived Monday evening. Only two days, she thought, and yet I feel as though I've been here for ages.

She ruminated on that as she drove back to the inn. She wondered if Thomas was home yet. That she didn't know where his room was struck her as odd. It seemed like something she should know, though she couldn't for the life of her say why. Maybe because she was coming to take such a proprietary interest in this elegant old house, Katy thought as she parked the car. It just seemed so *right* to come back here every night.

"You're weird, Katy," she muttered, swinging lightly across the porch.

As usual, excitement skittered along her nerves as she stepped inside. She had left the club early, pleading weariness. Which was true; she was so tired her legs trembled. But it was not the life-sapping fatigue that had plagued her for so long.

She stood still, listening for sounds of occupancy. Only the soft ticking of a clock disturbed the silence. Apparently, she was alone. She went into the kitchen to get one of the cold drinks she'd stashed in the refrigerator. Glancing out the dining-room window, she noticed the empty carport. Where was he? The question stung with its intensity.

Too restless to watch television, she sat on the couch for a while, leafing through a magazine. She told herself she wasn't waiting for him. But her gaze was drawn to the portrait hanging over the fireplace. The man now, like the man in the picture, still had that air of openness and integrity. He was a charmer by nature, but he didn't pour it on, she'd give him that.

He didn't seem too impressed with himself, either, for all that considerable charm. Just accepted as natural that women fell all over themselves for a smile from him, she thought, making a face.

She returned to the kitchen to deposit the cola can in the recycling carton. The room was neat and clean, as was the rest of the house. The maid's work, she supposed. She hadn't yet met Maddie. Out too early in the morning, in too late at night.

Increasingly restive, she wandered out to the deck. It was chilly enough for a sweater but she had left hers inside. She hugged herself. Lights were coming down the road. Her heart gave a wild leap. It had to be him; the road dead-ended here. He drove into the carport and she was caught in the glare of his headlights, her slim frame outlined before he switched them off.

For a brief moment, Katy imagined that she had the right to be here waiting for him, the right to welcome him home with eager arms. The truck door opened. Swiftly, she shook off the dangerously seductive thought.

"Well, hello," he said, getting out. "What are you doing standing out here in the dark?"

"Enjoying the night." She rubbed her arms.

"And freezing." He came up beside her. "Here, take my jacket, I have a sweater on under it."

She stood perfectly still while he wrapped the light garment around her shoulders. It smelled of him and her nostrils flared with pleasure.

Thomas slipped her silky hair from under the jacket's collar. The subtle perfume she wore gifted him with the scent of roses, the delicate pink ones that haunt soft, summer nights. Inhaling deeply, he took his hands from her and leaned against a pillar to study the moon. He'd made a point of telling himself that he had exaggerated the powerful attraction he had to her. Well, he was wrong. If anything, he hadn't credited just how powerful it really was.

He felt an urgent need to pull her into his arms and taste whatever it was that simmered between them. But he was a sensitive man and could feel the wariness in her.

"I had dinner tonight with Patsy and her friend Ken." Katy broke the taut silence.

"I know Ken."

"I suppose you know everyone on the island."

"Just about."

Undeterred by his terseness, she asked, "Date tonight?"

"Yes."

"Serious?"

"No." The night darkened as clouds occluded the moon. Absently, Thomas adjusted the jacket around her delicate shoulders. "Why have you been avoiding me?" he asked abruptly.

She stiffened. The heavy beat of a moment passed before she sighed and said, "You know why, Thomas."

"Maybe. But I'd like to hear it from you."

"Because of what happens when we're together," she said evenly.

He stepped closer. "And what's that?"

Her chin snapped up. "Don't toy with me, Thomas. You know what I'm talking about, you've felt it, too."

"Yes, I have. And do. But *I'm* not afraid of it."

"Neither am I."

God, that mouth, he thought, that soft, red, deliciously stubborn mouth! "Aren't you?" he asked, low and husky.

"No, I am not," she retorted. "I'm simply averse to—to following it to its natural conclusion."

His own mouth curved ever so slightly. "I see."

Tension thrummed between them, deep and hot and exciting. So exciting, Katy thought, tensing as his body swayed toward hers. She swallowed as he touched her hair.

"Well, at least you admit it is a natural conclusion," he remarked after a short pause, and tucked an unruly curl behind her ear. "You have anything serious going in California?"

"No," she said too quickly. "I mean, yes. The, uh, decision is still pending."

"Which means it isn't serious. If it was, you'd be there with him, not here with me." Thomas smiled in wry amusement at his relief. "Maybe he's just not right for you."

"He's exactly right for me," Katy countered. Having created a suitor out of thin air, she felt compelled to defend him. "He's really quite wonderful and we have many things in common."

"Maybe so, but my opinion of him still holds. The man's a fool, to let you leave him."

Her lips curved with a quick, impish smile. "Well, Thomas, I don't recall asking his permission."

He laughed, making no effort to mask the pleasure he took in her insouciant rebuke. "Ah, I stand corrected. Do you love him?"

His question let all the air out of her balloon. Sighing, she pushed at her hair. "No. Actually, there isn't anyone *to* love, in California, or anywhere else. Well, my accountant's crazy about me, but he rather resembles Harpo Marx and sprays spittle when he gets excited, so..." His laugh ambushed her. "I just made up the rest of it," she confessed.

"Why?"

"Instinct, maybe. Wisdom unaware..." She looked up at him, her expression sweetly earnest. "Maybe I'm wrong, but I think you're becoming interested in me and that disturbs me. Well, I don't return that interest, Thomas. Damn, this is awkward." She sighed. "Look, you seem to be a really nice guy and I just... just don't want anyone getting hurt, that's all."

"So you made up a serious suitor to thwart me, stop me in my tracks, so to speak?" His eyes danced.

"So to speak, yes. Well, I didn't make up my accountant, no one could make up *him*." She waited out his quick laugh. "Look, I want to be completely honest with you, okay? I like you, I find you attractive, but I'm not in the market for a relationship, no matter how short-term." She shivered and clutched the coat collar tighter. "Let's go in, shall we? I'm cold."

Inside the warm kitchen, she handed him his jacket with a brief word of thanks and immediately started upstairs.

"You're right, you know," he said, leaning against the shining mahogany handrail. "I am interested. Very interested. And I don't believe for a minute that you don't return that interest."

She stopped dead and he could see her draw herself up haughtily. Ah, the eternal thrill of the chase, he thought. Did it ever fade? Just the way she turned and looked at him with that aristocratic tilt of the head was a delicious stimulant. He adored it!

The breath she drew lifted her breasts and threw back her shoulders. Her velvety, violet gaze touched his upturned face, feature by feature. "I've already said I find you attractive. Sexy, to be blunt. So to that degree, I do return your interest. But that's not a very high degree, Thomas. So thanks, but no thanks. All I want here is peace and quiet."

Thomas punched out a breath. Okay, her rejection stung, but not too much; he could read between the lines. Even her stance challenged his manhood, he thought, shifting. When he met her narrowed gaze, he had to forcibly restrain his hot-blooded urge to take up that challenge, to hold that defiant mouth against his until it melted into the sweetness he could almost taste on his tongue. Careful, he warned himself. There's deep water here, water you could drown in. And he'd love nothing better. Damn!

He smiled, his voice gentling. "Message taken and noted, Katy."

She nodded and hurried upstairs. She didn't trust herself to remain with him an instant longer.

She didn't bother locking her door. In fact, she hadn't locked it after that first night. A measure of trust, she supposed. She had no fear that he'd come tearing in to assault her. Katy conceded a quick smile.

Amusement faded as she took off her clothes and looked in the mirror. Her cheeks were flushed, her eyes still sparkling with temper and its companion, desire. The heat of it still burned where she ached to have him touch her.

Katy sighed as she acknowledged the real message he'd gotten. He knew how much she wanted him.

She took her tangle of ambivalent feelings to bed, where her mind insisted on rehashing every word. "Don't do this to yourself, Katy," she ordered, to no avail.

Closing her eyes, she yawned and curled into her favorite sleeping position. California was glutted with attractive males, she thought drowsily. Why was Thomas so different? Different from anyone she had ever met....

She slept deeply, yet her body twitched and jerked. Her mouth opened in a silent scream as memories churned within her active brain.

She was Karin; she was herself.

She was both, feeling it all, the gut-wrenching horror, the sensation of falling, falling, seeing the ground rushing up, hearing the fragility of metal and fabric hitting, bouncing, crumpling as the small plane met solid pavement. The Katy part of her ran down the runway, ran wildly, desperately, knowing she would never reach the wreck in time, knowing it was coming...

And then it did, a fountain of flames against the black sky!

The forceful explosion tossing her around like a rag doll... Terror and pain and a quilt of darkness spreading over her, smothering, heavy. Yet she struggled against it— she had to get up, had to reach the plane, had to help her sister! Karin! Where was Karin!

"Karin!"

The silent scream in her dream became reality, an anguished sound that shattered the night and brought her awake in a sobbing rush of horror.

Thomas was out of bed and running up the stairs before he was fully aware of what had happened.

He had time for one thought as he raced down the hallway—luckily he slept in pajama bottoms. But quick on the heels of that thought came another—Katy. Her sobs came through the door and he opened it without thought or hesitation.

By the light of the moon he could see her huddled in bed, weeping. He snapped on the lamp and did the only thing that made sense to him; he sat down on the edge of the bed and gathered her into his arms. Fiercely he held her, giving comfort, making shushing noises, pulling her closer until she was cradled in his embrace. She huddled against him, seemingly grateful for this shelter from whatever demons pursued her.

"Hush, now, it's all right," he murmured over and over again. Still she wept, huge, body-shaking sobs that tore at his heart. She felt so small in his arms, so fragile. What had frightened her? "Shh, now, it's all right."

At length her weeping stopped, although her body still shook. When he loosened his grasp, she clung to him. He nestled his face in her hair. "It's all right...all over now," he whispered, inhaling her clean, fresh scent.

Silence pooled around them. Thomas managed to reach some tissues without letting her go. He could feel her wiping her eyes, and he smiled when he heard her blow her nose. Quietly, he held her while she mastered the occasional hiccuping sob that still racked her throat. His own emotions were exceedingly strong and disconcerting. He felt fiercely protective, awesomely powerful.

Silence surrounded them. Wind lifted the curtains and blew over them with ripples of coolness. When she nestled closer, Thomas found himself in a predicament. At first meaning only to comfort, he was rapidly becoming aware that he held a soft, curvaceous woman clad only in a scrap of satin. Her lips touched his bare chest. His body jerked. This is what it probably feels like to be branded, he thought in confusion. Then she turned her face up to his and he stopped thinking.

He had even lost the capacity to reason, Thomas realized in some remote part of his brain as her mouth came to his. She was only reacting to the situation—he knew that! But he'd have to be a dead man not to respond. He took her lips with a passion that spun his head.

She moaned. A protest? Hunger blazed in him, causing wildfires to break out in dozens of places in his taut body, tempting his mind to deny even the possibility of protest.

He kissed her wet face, tasting saltiness, tasting sweetness.

He kissed her eyelids, and her lashes fluttered on his face like tiny butterflies.

Then he took her mouth again urgently.

Katy felt another moan well up. She half lay against him, her breasts thrusting into his bare chest, her stomach hard against his thighs. Desire shot through her from there down, making her press closer, as if she were trying to get into his skin with him. The searing union of lips was nearly her undoing. His tongue entangled hers and she knew intimately the taste and texture of him. She found dark, enticing mystery in the night-smell of skin, in the shape of his mouth. Caution was forgotten, fear but a breath on the wind. She wanted more . . . and more.

Thomas was raining kisses on her face, her eyelids, her lips. He groaned her name, just once, but the sound managed to pierce her fevered haze. She pulled away and flattened her palms against his chest. Their rapid breaths mingled as they stared at each other.

Katy was shocked at the response he had drawn from her. She sat back on her knees, her thoughts swimming. Were his? Did he feel as overwhelmed by this exchange of passion as she did? His face was impassive, but his eyes were intensely blue, stained with the heat of their embrace.

She held his gaze, hoping he would understand. "I'm very vulnerable right now, Thomas."

So am I, Katy! The words stopped at the edge of his tongue as Thomas gazed into wide violet eyes. He blew out his breath in a long whoosh of sound.

Her lovely face was still wet. Another muscle tightened, one in the vicinity of his heart. This time he grabbed the whole box of tissues and handed them to her.

"Thank you. Seems like I'm always thanking you," she said with a tremulous smile.

"Feel free." Marveling at his light voice, Thomas touched her cheek with the tips of his fingers. "What happened to cause those tears?"

"Bad dream."

"I guessed that. What was it about?"

Katy edged away from him as reason returned. "Just a dream."

"No, it wasn't. Tell me about it."

Her lashes fanned down and she lay back against the pillow. With what seemed like superhuman effort, Thomas stood up and pulled the comforter over her beautiful, sexy legs to her waist. Her hair tumbled over the snowy linen. He smoothed it gently with his hands. "Tell me, Katy."

Her soft mouth, reddened by his kisses, quirked downward at the corners. "You're very persuasive."

"So I'm told."

"Also a hard man to resist."

"Yeah, I am," he admitted with an unrepentant grin. He sat down on the edge of the bed. "Would you like me to stay with you a while?"

"Yes. It's stupid, but I'm still a little shaky inside."

"It's not stupid. Just human. What happened in the dream?"

Having found herself in yet another intimate position with him, Katy swallowed hard. He was too near. So was the dream. She took another moment, then said, "About nine months ago I was involved in a plane crash, and in the dream I'm back in the plane." A tremor ran through her slim body. "A plane that's falling from the sky, landing on one wing, tumbling over, crumpling. I keep reliving the accident, keep feeling that sensation of utter and absolute helplessness, keep seeing..." She faltered and hauled in a breath.

"My God." Thomas's hand had stilled in her hair, arrested by her flat voice as much as by her story. Emotions boiled within him as he put pictures to her words, tenderness rose in him until it was all he could do not to drag her back into the safety of his arms.

He blew out a breath. "Were you hurt?"

"Yes." Her voice thinned. "But I was lucky, I survived."

"God," he whispered, his imagination rioting. Nine months ago, she'd said. So that's why the haunted eyes. She was still recovering from that dreadful trauma.

"You all right now?" he asked abruptly.

"Yes, I'm fine. Physically, anyway." She seemed about to continue, then shook her head.

What else had she been going to say? Thomas wondered. He felt a sense of having missed something. At length he asked, "What kind of plane was it?"

"A small plane. Similar to the one I saw in the photograph on the mantelpiece."

Thomas glanced at her, but her lashes were lowered. "So that's why you drove here instead of flying."

"Yes. I haven't wanted to get near a plane since—since it happened."

She didn't embellish her comment, but her entangled fingers spoke volumes.

"Oh, Katy, that's perfectly understandable," he said urgently. "But honey, what happened to you is a once-in-a-lifetime experience. Statistics show—"

"I'm not interested in statistics!" Her lashes shot up, followed by a wan smile. "I'm sorry, Thomas, I know you're only trying to help."

"Yes, I am. I want to help, Katy, and I think I can." His voice was still edged with urgency.

Her immediate response was a sharp shake of her head. "Lots of people have tried to help, and failed. I'm just too afraid to even think of flying," she said dismissively. Another attempt at a smile twisted her lips. "I guess my screaming woke you? I apologize for that. It doesn't happen often. Usually I'm able to wake up before the dream gets bad. Anyway, I guess you're my hero. So thank you again, hero," she added with a valiant attempt at lightness.

"Hero, huh? I'll buy that." He wanted her to continue about the dream, but her eyes warned him off. They also warned him that their passionate interlude was not open to discussion.

His gaze lingered on her face as emotions warred within him. She had basically told him to back off. He knew he wouldn't. Because he couldn't. *Synchronicity* he thought, savoring the word.

"You said the plane *fell*. What do you mean? Did it lose power, did the engine cut out?"

"Faulty equipment, they said. I wasn't there when . . ." she trailed off sadly.

Thomas gave her a sharp look. "You weren't there? I don't understand."

Katy bit down on her lip as she realized what she'd done. So completely had she identified with her twin sister that it had become *her* trauma. In her mind, she had been in that plane.

"Thomas, I . . . what I told you isn't exactly the way it happened. I mean, it wasn't me in that plane. But it might as well have been, I felt every single second of that crash!" Her head lowered. "It's very hard to explain."

"Try," he said softly.

"My sister was the one who died in that plane. But I . . . I was waiting for her near the edge of the runway, waiting to pick her up that evening and bring her h-home." Katy dashed at tears. "We were twins, you see, and well, there's always been this sort of special mental/emotional communication between us. Once she fell and broke her arm and I *felt* it, Thomas. My arm hurt so much they had to sedate me until *her* pain stopped. So when I say I experienced the crash, I meant it. I felt her fear, her horror. And all the while, I was running, trying to reach the plane before it exploded."

"Oh, God, it exploded?"

"Yes. That's how I sustained my injuries, from the force of the blast. Mercifully, I blacked out then." She bowed her head. "Oh, God, Thomas, I should have been with her! I intended to make that flight—we'd planned to stay overnight in Reno, and have some fun. But something came up and I had to cancel out. So she died alone. And I'm still alive."

"Guilt, too, huh?" he said, shaking his head.

"Tons of it." She tried a smile, a shrug. "But I'm coping with it, as best I can. Thank you, Thomas, for being such a good listener."

"Anytime." Standing, he asked gruffly, "You okay now?"

"I'm okay." Her head lifted. "I really am."

Thomas touched the point of her chin, his movements suddenly awkward. It was strange, he thought, this feeling of wanting to leave, wanting even more to stay. He removed his hand, straightened to tall sternness.

"Good," he said. "Go back to sleep now." *Something I'm not going to do easily,* he predicted as he turned out the light and left the room.

Later, lying in his own bed in a welter of confusion, his prediction proved true. Every time he replayed the scene, thought about her story again, he felt turned inside out. No wonder her eyes were haunted.

He had to try to help, of course. His nature, if nothing else, guaranteed it. Her coming here to the island—to *him*—was no accident, he felt sure of that. He'd tell her so tomorrow. She would see that he could help. If she'd let him. Dammit, she had to accept his help! He had no doubt about that. Great gobs of tenderness still tightened his chest whenever he remembered her desolate weeping.

Oh, and the way she'd clung to him! The way her body felt clasped in his arms. Incredibly soft and curvy. The taste of her. And the way she smelled—why did women smell so wonderful at night?

For a moment, his mind stumbled on the warning she'd issued earlier in the evening. *I'm not in the market for a relationship, no matter how short-term. Just not interested, Thomas.* Because she was afraid I'd get hurt, he thought, smiling as he remembered her expression, so sweetly earnest, so vulnerable and appealing...

Desire replaced the tenderness as he pictured again the garment she wore to bed. Tiny nothing that it was, he could have skimmed it over her head with no trouble at all.

His palms itched. And there was a sweet little ache in his chest where she'd rested her head. He wasn't the least bit sleepy. Defeated, he snapped on the light and reached for his book.

Katy moved through the gray morning light with a silken sense of lightness. The leaden sadness in her heart had eased somewhat. Although she loved rainy days, something much more elemental heightened her spirits. Each

time she thought of Thomas's tenderness the night before, a warmth moved within her. He had been so gentle,
so considerate. It was tempting to go back through each
separate sensation he had aroused in that brief time, to
drag it out, explore every sparkling facet.

She resisted temptation.

It was going to be awkward enough facing him this
morning.

Had he understood why she had turned to him last
night? Had he realized that in some instinctive way she was
reaffirming her own life by simply feeling alive? Alive with
every sense she possessed, Katy admitted with a long, slow
stretch of supple muscles.

And she had changed her mind about the weather. She
wanted to take pictures today. As if on cue, a shaft of
sunshine fell across her face. It was raining and the sun was
shining. What was that old saying? "The devil's beating
his wife." Chuckling, Katy raced down the hall to the
bathroom.

After her shower, she pulled on jeans and a classic white
shirt, which she belted with a chain of silver shells. Silver
circles hung from her small earlobes. Mascara, a fluff of
powder across her nose and a peachy lip gloss were all the
makeup she needed. Taking a denim jacket from the
closet—it was cool this morning—she went downstairs to
the kitchen.

The cat—named Trouble—lay on a round rug beside the
table. At least this cat was tame, Katy thought, eyeing the
long, lean figure standing in front of the sink.

"Good morning," Thomas said, turning to greet her.
He took in her fitted jeans and shirt in one glance. "Coffee's hot."

"Oh, good." Katy paused inside the kitchen door to
calm the sudden flurry of her pulse. He was clad in
matching navy blue shirt and trousers, and he looked
wonderful.

"Why you named that cat Trouble is beyond me, all he does is sleep," she remarked.

"That's during the day. Nights..." He shook his head, his eyes crinkling. "He roams the hills and valleys looking for love."

Delightedly Katy laughed. God, she did like this man!

He handed her a cup of coffee. "I'm afraid you're on your own for breakfast, I've got an early-morning appointment. There are eggs and bacon in the fridge."

She nodded, sipped her coffee. What was that early-morning appointment? Was he flying today? She didn't want to know.

"Who painted the portrait?" she asked idly. "The one over the fireplace."

"My grandmother. She's quite well known for her portraits. Nina Logan?"

Katy shook her head apologetically. "Sorry, I don't recognize the name. But then, we didn't have much to do with portraits and such when I was young. It's very good, though. I can see why you keep it there."

Thomas reddened. The portrait was both an embarrassment and a treasure. He was going to have to rehang the blessed thing. Maybe in his office.

"It's also valuable," he said stiffly. "If you want to wait half an hour, Maddie will be here to fix your breakfast. I'm sorry about the rain, it does dampen a vacation."

Humor slanted the violet eyes watching him over the rim of her cup. "I can take care of my own breakfast. And I like rainy days, I like the cocooning instinct it evokes."

His fingers tightened around his own cup as Thomas imagined cocooning with her. He possessed a healthy male ego and her mouth was a saucy curve that needed to be kissed.

Things had changed between them, he realized. Things had definitely changed. For better or worse remained to be seen.

Remembering the nature of his appointment, he scratched his head in consternation. How did she feel about him being a pilot?

"Thomas, I apologize for last night," she was saying.

He stared at her, trying to get a grip on his thoughts. "You what?"

"Apologize. For the trouble I caused, waking you up like that. I'm so embarrassed . . ."

"Don't be ridiculous."

Her head went back. "What?"

"I said, don't be ridiculous."

"I wasn't aware I was being ridiculous, I was simply trying to apologize for bothering you last night," she snapped.

"There you go again!" He glared at her, his jaw tight. "Last night was no bother. I'd have to be a real jerk to find it *bothersome.*"

Katy stared her amazement; what were they fighting about? "I'm sorry, I was just . . ." She lifted her shoulders in a helpless shrug.

"Me, too." Thomas drained his cup, scalding his tongue in the process. What the hell was he getting so fired up about? The smile he offered was pained and wry. "I'm not usually this grumpy in the mornings, but I didn't get much sleep last night."

"Which is exactly why I was trying to apologize."

"Katy!" Amusement twinkled in his eyes and erupted in a laugh. "Okay, apology accepted."

"It's about time." Katy poured another cup of coffee. The sound of his laughter had lit sparklers somewhere inside her.

"Where are you off to this morning?" she asked.

"The airport. I'm flying to Portland. A charter flight."

Of course, Katy thought. That's a uniform he's wearing. She leaned back against the counter. Another sip of coffee handily prevented her from responding. Her gaze bemused, she watched him shrug into his jacket.

What would it be like to be the wife of a pilot? *Your stomach knotted with apprehension, fear like a brick in your throat every time he left for the airport,* she answered herself with a deep, inward tremor. No woman could live with that. At least this one couldn't. Her throat hurt.

He picked up the captain's hat lying on the counter behind him. "What are you going to do today?" he asked.

She waved a hand. "Oh, I don't know, just go where the mood moves me, I suppose."

"Just be sure it moves you back here." Thomas hesitated, then squared his shoulders. "Katy, I have some free time later on. Why don't you meet me at the airport about noon and look over my plane, maybe even take a ride in it?"

Four

Katy stared at him for the space of three thunderous heartbeats. She couldn't believe that he would consider her fears so inconsequential as to dismiss them outright. She couldn't believe how much that hurt. As if to fill the sinking sensation in her stomach, she drank deeply of her coffee. Shiny violet eyes met his for a searing instant before her lashes veiled them again.

"Just like that, hmm? Just hop into your plane and away we go?" Her bright tone was heavily at odds with her pinched features.

Thomas winced. He had thought the risk worth taking. Now he wasn't so sure. "No, not 'just like that,'" he said gruffly. "I'll help you, Katy."

"You can't help me." Her chin snapped up. "Besides, I didn't ask for your help. My problems don't involve you. So why you feel free to stick your nose into my personal business—"

"You didn't have to ask! Good grief, Katy, you woke up screaming and crying in the night. I held and comforted you, I was involved—I *am* involved, damn it!" His voice quieted. "And I really can help you."

She was all emotion, crying inside, striving for calmness outside. "Sure you can," she said huskily. "You'll just wave your magic wand and all my silly little fears will fade away, right, Thomas? Because, of course, they *are* silly little fears."

"No, they're not silly and they're not little."

"That's what you implied."

His nostrils flared as he noted the ice in her voice. "Damn it, Katy!" he began, then inwardly groaned at the way he was handling the situation. "I didn't mean to imply any such thing. I only meant—"

"I know what you meant, I've heard it often enough," she said with a stinging touch of bitterness. "'Oh, come on, Katy, there's nothing to be afraid of—the chance of another accident is one in a million!'" she mimicked.

"There's some truth in that," Thomas said. "Flying is far safer than driving. There are five hundred times more fatal car accidents than plane crashes. Comparing an average of ninety flight fatalities a year versus over a hundred a *day* on our national highways—"

"Statistics again. Throwing numbers at me, as if that's going to make any difference!" She set down her cup with an audible snap. "Do you honestly think you can undo what months of intensive therapy couldn't?"

"You had therapy?"

"Yes, I had therapy. Hours and hours of therapy. But it didn't help. Every time I try to fly, I panic." Her glistening eyes flicked his face like tiny whips. "Do you know what panic is, Thomas? It is the acute and overwhelming feeling of imminent danger." The hurt had ballooned with each passing moment. Her voice was raw. "And I have every right to feel that way!"

"Katy, I know that." Thomas raised his hands in appeal. "Just listen to me, let me tell you why I—"

"No, let me finish telling *you!* Then we'll be done with it." She drew herself up very straight. "Your precious statistics also show that there are at least twenty-five million people who are fearful flyers to some degree, so I'm not alone. But in my case, my fear is based on real danger, a danger that actually happened, to my sister. To *me,* Thomas. Not in some newspaper account or on the evening news. You can't imagine—" She was choking on words now. "You just can't *imagine* what it's like to stand helplessly by and watch someone you love burn to death! So you can take your statistics and your advice and—and just leave me alone!"

Wheeling, Katy ran from the kitchen and up the stairs to her room. She heard Thomas call her name with an urgency that would have stopped her had she not been near tears. But she was through with him, she thought furiously.

"Oh, Katy, you idiot! How can you be through with him, when you haven't even started!" she groaned. Smothering a hysterical laugh, she sat down in the rocker and let the blessed tears come. They seemed to come more easily these days. For months after the plane crash, they had pooled into a hard, jagged knot at the back of her throat, until she thought she was swallowing a chunk of ice. She'd felt frozen then, empty and joyless. But now...

She wiped her eyes. "Well, not frozen," she muttered ironically. Even her skin burned.

She rocked, soothed by the rhythmic movement, until she could think more clearly. Did Thomas think she *enjoyed* this fear? she thought wretchedly. Besides being cowardly, it was an enormous inconvenience. Her work often included long-distance travel, and flying was the quickest, most sensible way to achieve that.

Except that she wasn't sensible about flying. Not even rational about it, she thought bleakly. Therapy had given her more understanding and a great deal more patience with herself. Even so, it wasn't easy living with self-imposed limitations.

A sudden soft tap on the door stilled her heart.

"Katy?" Thomas called.

Instantly, she was caught up in a tempestuous swirl of emotions again! How could he do that? she wondered furiously.

"Yes?" she barely managed to respond.

"I'd like to finish what I was saying. Please, open the door?"

She rose from the chair, walked across the room and opened it, her expression wary.

He stepped inside.

She sat back down and folded her hands in her lap.

"You don't make this easy," Thomas remarked.

Silence. Only those wary violet eyes were communicating with him, and he didn't like what they were saying. Doggedly he carried on. "Katy, the reason I felt free to 'stick my nose in your business' is because your problems do affect me. I think you're here for a reason."

She frowned. "Oh, come on, Thomas—"

"Please, just hear me out?" he requested, plowing a hand through his hair. "I feel strongly that your decision to come to the islands—and to me—is no coincidence. Coincidence is accidental, just chance, and I don't believe in either. I believe in synchronicity, which is the falling into place of the natural order of things."

He drew an empowering breath. "And to me, nothing could be more natural than having you enter my life at your greatest time of need. Because I *can* help you, Katy. I firmly believe that."

Her hands slid over her face and through her hair, lifting the golden tresses and letting them fan through her

fingers before she sighed and murmured, "Oh, Thomas."
She looked up at him. "I know you believe that, I know
you're sincere. But I also know myself. With all due respect to your beliefs, they do not reflect mine," she said
quietly. "My purpose for coming to the islands is exactly
what I told you, no more, no less. That's all there is to it."
A tiny smile softened her mouth. "I do appreciate your
concern, though. Thank you, I guess."

"You're welcome, I guess." Thomas plowed another
furrow through his hair, then sighed and looked at his
watch. "I have to leave now, but I'll be home around five-
thirty. We'll talk some more then."

He thought his tone sounded fine—firm, authoritative.
But Katy's face immediately closed against it.

"We have nothing more to talk about," she said crisply.
She got up and opened the door wider, an obvious invitation for him to get the hell out of her room, Thomas acknowledged.

"I think we do." He stepped out the door. "I'll see you
around five-thirty."

"I don't know yet what my plans are for the evening,
but very likely I'll spend it with Patsy. Bye, Thomas." The
door closed behind him with a firm little *click*.

Feeling itchy with frustration, Thomas clamped his lips
together to keep back a searing oath. Her dismissal hurt.
It hurt much more than it should have. Good grief, he
thought, closing his eyes, on top of everything else, I'm
infatuated with the woman. He made himself laugh—a
hormone-ridden teenager, at his age! He said through the
door, "Well, if you're here, okay, if not . . ." She didn't
answer. Oh, hell. He turned and took the stairs two at a
time.

By the time she arrived at Patsy's showroom, Katy's
mood matched the sky. Every time she replayed the scene
with Thomas, she felt as if she'd failed some important

test. The idea that she had been sent here by fate, as it were, was impossible to take seriously. But he had been serious. Well, there was no accounting for other people's beliefs, she thought irritably.

Growing impatient with herself, she shoved him to the back of her mind and concentrated on the task at hand, which was creating a more effective display of Patsy's beautiful pottery.

She giggled as Patsy cussed a wooden board that had pinched her fingers. "Darned thing," she grumbled, a scowl on her freckled face. "What's wrong with the way I had it, anyway?"

"Patsy, it looked like you stood back and just tossed things in this general direction. Now, come on, hand me that board and the one beside it. We're going to organize this place," Katy said. *I wish Thomas wasn't flying today!*

She licked her lips and set the board on concrete blocks, one and then another, to form some crude shelving. Over this she spread a swath of pearl-gray velvet. *He's probably in the air right now.* Annoyed by her runaway thoughts, she focused her attention on arranging her friend's wares, repositioning each piece until she was pleased with the eye-catching result.

Soon Patsy drifted into the kitchen and produced a sea-food salad. Not really hungry, Katy nibbled at it. She wondered if she would be home tonight when Thomas came in. Home. Not your home, she reminded herself sternly. Not your man, either. Even though you want him—all of him, the arrogant part, the humorous, considerate and thoughtless parts that make up a very desirable male.

He had called her "honey." Curious how that common little word kept softening her heart. Granted, he had hurt her. But he hadn't meant to. Katy sighed. Now she was making allowances for him.

While Patsy gathered up the leftovers, Katy carried their plates to the sink and stood for a moment looking out the window. Mist hovered over the hilltops and nested in the valleys. Visibility was very low. He was probably in the air right now. Wasn't it dangerous to fly in this kind of weather?

A shiver shuddered through her. Katy frowned, discomfited by her uneasy state of mind. She was worrying about a man she hardly knew.

"Does Thomas always fly in this kind of soup?" she asked Patsy with a casual air.

"Yep. He's one of those fly-by-the-seat-of-the-pants pilots, loves to challenge the sky."

"Oh, God. A daredevil."

Patsy gave her a keen look. "Hey, come on, honey, lighten up," she said softly. "Thomas is no daredevil. He's an excellent pilot. And a serious one, too. He really is, Katy."

"I didn't mean to put him down, I just . . . wondered."

"That's really a problem, isn't it?" Patsy said softly. "His being a pilot."

"Well, it's not something I'm comfortable with," she said. "But it's hardly a *problem,* Patsy. I'm not going to be here long enough to get involved, with Thomas or anyone else."

"Katy, he's the right man for you, I feel it in my bones," Patsy said earnestly.

"And we both know how infallible your bones are!" Katy hooted. "Look, Patsy, if I want a man, well, hey, there's always my accountant!"

Patsy gave an inelegant snort. "Placid City."

"True, we're not exactly Tristan and Isolde, but . . ." Katy glanced at her, eyes agleam with mischief. "He's a great kisser."

"Hah! Not only do I doubt he's a great kisser, I doubt he's even in the running."

"I'm not in the running, either, so what's the problem?" Chuckling at her friend's pained look, Katy walked back to the messy showroom. "Okay, hand me those small pieces. You know, these resemble Quamper Ware," she said, eager to get on to a less provocative subject.

Still grumbling, Patsy obliged her. The two women worked through the afternoon setting up the showroom to Katy's satisfaction. Then she took photographs of each piece and promised her friend copies.

"Oh, good! I can post some of them at my friend's shop in Friday Harbor. Hey, I know what, let's have dinner together tonight, Ken and me, you and Thomas," Patsy suggested. "He and Ken like each other, so it should be great fun. And that's our goal, you said," she reminded Katy. "Fun!"

Katy managed to look amused. "True. But what makes you think I want to have dinner with Thomas?"

"You really don't like him?"

"Well, of course I like him, he's a likeable person. All right, all right, *very* likeable," she conceded. "But I, well, I just think it would be better not to socialize with him."

"Better, my foot," Patsy scoffed. "Safer is more like it."

Part of Katy agreed, which made the other part of her indignant. She could certainly spend an evening in Thomas Logan's company without ending up in his bed. "Prudent," she compromised.

"Prudent? Oh, for heaven's sake, Katy, one bad marriage does not qualify you for martyrhood. Look at me, I've been through two of 'em, and I'm certainly not concerned with being prudent."

"Well, maybe I don't take things as lightly as you, Patsy."

"Well, maybe you ought to," Patsy retorted.

"Okay, maybe I should, but..." Katy laughed and shook her head. "I'm just not made that way. Anyway, this whole discussion is academic. Thomas and I had a fight this morning, so I doubt he'd care to take me to dinner.''

"You take him, then."

Katy looked exasperated. "Didn't you hear what I just said?"

"Sure I did. But Thomas doesn't hold grudges. Besides, he likes a good fight."

"He does? Well, I don't," Katy said, firmly squashing the thrill inside her. "Besides, he's got some weird idea that I was *sent* here, by fate, no less. Because he can help me solve all my problems," she added, looking amused at his fanciful notion.

"Maybe he can. Our Thomas is sagacious as well as sexy."

Katy shrugged. "Well, the sexy part I can't dispute. He might already have plans for tonight, you know."

"So tell him to change them," Patsy said so reasonably that Katy felt a giggle crowd her throat.

Keenly aware of her inconsistencies, she replied tartly, "I doubt that Thomas Logan takes orders from anyone."

Patsy just looked wise.

Katy bit her lip. She was being outmaneuvered. But not by Patsy. By herself. Still, Thomas had extended her many small kindnesses, well beyond those of a host. *Far beyond,* she reflected, unaware that she was smiling. Taking him to dinner could be considered a small token of her appreciation.

"All right, I'll ask him." She sighed. "I suppose it's better than being a third wheel with you and Ken again."

Patsy cast her an oblique glance, but held her tongue. They agreed to meet at Ken's club at seven, with or without Thomas. "It'll be fun," Patsy decreed.

"Of course it will!" Laughing, Katy gave her bubbly friend a fierce hug before hurrying to her car.

Katy drove home—to Thomas's house, she corrected—
so distractedly it was a wonder she made all the right turns.

His housekeeper was just leaving when she arrived. A
large, square woman with a crop of short, salt-and-pepper
curls, Maddie waited on the porch, plainly curious. She
looked Katy over with black eyes that seemed to pierce the
skin and see right into the heart.

"So you're Katy," she said. "I'm Maddie Wills. I heard
about you." Another frank appraisal. "You really are
pretty as a picture."

What had Maddie heard about her? And who had said
she was pretty as a picture? Thomas? The thought sent
velvet tingles down her spine.

"You like that boy of mine, do you?" Maddie asked.

"Uh, you mean Thomas?" Katy asked, feeling off balance.

Maddie's mouth softened. "Only boy I got," she said.
"Used to tan his britches when he'd come here to stay with
his grandma and grandpa. Orneriest kid you ever seen."
Black eyes sparkled. "Sure grew into a fine man, though,
didn't he!"

"Yes, he did. Well, nice to finally meet you, Maddie,"
Katy said brightly. "If you'll excuse me, I have to dress for
dinner."

A laugh bubbled through her lips as she scurried into the
house. *Orneriest kid you ever seen!* Oh, Thomas!

There were fresh flowers on her dresser. Maddie, she
supposed. Thomas's orders? Another nice thought. Sitting down on the bed to take off her sneakers, she let her
mind stray to last night, and a wave of the most delicious
warmth enveloped her. She recalled vividly the gentleness
of his hands as he held her, his low, tender, soothing voice.
The sun-bronzed skin that tasted so good to her lips. The
hunger in his kiss...

Distracted anew, she stripped off her clothes, put on her robe and went to the bathroom to bathe in wisteria-scented water.

A steamy half hour later, she floated around her bedroom as nude and rosy as a baby's bottom. A quick check out the window revealed lowering clouds, but no rain. Relieved, she brushed and blow-dried her freshly shampooed hair.

Skirt or dress, Patsy had decreed; the restaurant she'd chosen merited a touch of glamour. Katy selected a full skirt of handkerchief linen with a fringe of scalloped lace around the hem. With it she paired a sleeveless white crepe de chine blouse. Gold sparkled at her throat, and a blue and lavender cloth belt encircled her waist. She slipped on Italian leather pumps and surveyed herself in the mirror. Her eyes reflected doubt. The questions she had ignored earlier suddenly popped up again. What if Thomas didn't want to go to dinner with her? Or what if he really did have other plans?

Anxiety dug a hollow in her stomach. "Oh, for heaven's sake, Katy! It's no big deal," she muttered. Certainly not. If he didn't come with her, she'd just go by herself. And while rejection might sting, it wouldn't kill her.

But what if he came home to do just what he'd said this morning, to talk? She didn't feel like talking, not about that thorny subject, anyway. She still felt too many ragtags of emotion to discuss it with ease. Besides, there was nothing left to discuss.

"Enough what ifs, Kathleen," she advised herself firmly. She glanced at the clock. Nearly six-thirty. Another kind of anxiety began gnawing at her belly. Where was he? Was he a punctual man or given to tardiness? Had the weather delayed him?

Had he had a safe flight?

She shuddered, and hurriedly shoved the question back into its cave.

The sound of his truck broke across her thoughts like sunshine. Katy took a deep breath. Just a simple dinner with friends, she told herself. No big deal. Overlooking her erratic heartbeat, she walked downstairs.

He was coming in the back door as she descended the last step. They met in the living room. She made a small gesture of greeting.

Thomas returned the gesture. He had wanted her to be waiting for him. And here she was. All dressed up. Was she going somewhere?

"You're all dressed up," he said. Brilliant, Logan!

"Yes."

"You're going out?"

"Yes."

Disappointment shut down his brain. "Where?"

Her lashes lifted to give him the full effect of her eyes.

"I'm taking you to dinner."

Her tone was light, her manner superbly confident. But the uncertain look in her eyes betrayed her. Thomas was astounded at the tangled mass of emotions rampaging through his suddenly weightless body. *You're an infatuated fool, Logan.*

"Where are you taking me?" he asked, grinning idiotically.

"First to Ken's restaurant, where we'll meet him and Patsy, then to another place where, Patsy tells me, they serve fabulous salmon. You have twenty minutes to shower and dress," she said firmly.

Her stern warning delighted him. Suddenly, he leaned down and touched his mouth to hers in an impulsive kiss.

She took a quick breath. "Thank you, that was nice." Stepping away from him, she tapped her watch.

"You make me crazy, you know that?" Laughing, Thomas bounded down the hallway to his bedroom. He felt wonderful as well as crazy, and it was all because of her.

Why did *this* woman affect him so completely? Why not some uncomplicated beauty who bothered him not at all from the waist up? Katy bothered him all over. What made her so captivating? He would have to give the answer to that question some thought later on. Right now, he had a date to keep.

He was in the shower before his mind switched to the set-to they'd had this morning. Wrong as he had been to confront her like that, he'd meant well. He had a plan, of course, if only she would listen to him. But she had thought he was making light of her fear. If anything, he was impatient with it. He so loved the miracle of flying that it was hard to conceive that others were actually afraid of it. So he had tried to smother her protests with logic and statistics. Wrong again. Then he had tried to convince her with what she obviously considered so much mumbo jumbo.

"You screwed up royally, my lad," he growled as he turned off the water and grabbed a towel. But he felt too good to worry about that now. He would make it up to her, explain himself, maybe even apologize, later. Right now he had a whole evening ahead of him, with her at his side.

And who knew how that evening might end?

He raked through his closet to find something to wear. He wasn't a clotheshorse, but he did have a nice wardrobe. Why, then, was the tie he finally chose so gosh-awful with this tan-and-blue-striped shirt? A white shirt, he decided, ripping off the striped one. A man couldn't go wrong with a white shirt. And a pale blue blazer and gray slacks. The tie was just awful, period. Why in the world had he bought the thing! He jerked it off, scowled at his image, then burst out laughing. He was acting like a teenager on his first date! No, worse than that. Never had he been so picky about his clothes. But he wanted to please her. He'd pleased a lot of women in his lifetime, with very little effort, if the truth be known. This one, though, this one was *important*.

Why? Could this preposterous swirl of emotions be more than he suspected? Could it be love? Nonsense! People didn't fall in love this quick. You had to know the person for a long while, didn't you? But he felt as if he'd known her a thousand years. His stomach clenched like a fist—just the *thought* of loving her was scary!

Simmer down, Logan. He didn't believe in love at first sight, never mind that he'd been tied in knots since he'd first laid eyes on her. He believed in real love, though. With his parents and his grandparents as examples, how could he not? But at thirty-five, he secretly doubted it would ever happen to him. And it hadn't, he told himself. What he had was a severe case of lust, compounded by an even more severe case of infatuation.

"It may be painful, but it won't kill you," he assured his suave reflection.

He decided he didn't need a tie. Opening his shirt collar, Thomas strolled down the stairs to the living room where she sat waiting. Her gilded head was bent over a magazine. She had crossed her legs, and they were the kind of legs that could really mess up a man's head. He smiled, recalling her denial of needing anyone. *That* he could understand; apparently she had been badly hurt by some fool. But the rest of it...

Well, I don't return that interest, Thomas, she had said. Hah! he thought. She was interested, all right. And when that soft, silken sensuality she radiated caught fire... He cleared his throat.

"Ready?" he asked, holding his hand out to her.

Katy looked up at his query, and smiled as her gaze swept over his tall frame.

"Ready." She took his hand, liking his firm grip. An impish twinkle lit her eyes. "You look gorgeous, Thomas."

Inordinately pleased, he grinned. "Thank you. You look gorgeous, too. Have you thought about having those legs insured?"

"Not often," she returned so dryly he laughed.

Sobering, Thomas took her other hand, too. "Friends, Katy?" he asked softly. Her answer was suddenly very important.

"Friends, Thomas," Katy replied with a sweet sense of reprieve. Just dinner with friends, she told herself again, with more conviction this time. Freeing her hands, she gathered up her cashmere shawl and they walked to the door then left the house.

A dark green sports car resided in the garage. He opened the door for her, Katy noted. Such chivalry seemed a lost art in her California circle.

Conversation on the short drive was kept to social chatter. She had a rich laugh, and Thomas found himself growing wittier by the minute just to hear it. He had a million questions swarming his mind, but he managed, by sheer willpower, to contain them. She had lowered her guard with him, and he was determined to give her no cause to regret it.

Ken's Club was already crowded when they arrived, a new band tuning up, smoke and noise in equal proportions creating a pulsating haze above the crowd.

"My goodness, look at all the people," Katy said as they joined her friends.

"Tourists, God love 'em!" Patsy said. She grinned at Thomas. "You are an absolute hunk," she informed him.

Thomas laughed and kissed her cheek. Katy felt envious, and even a little jealous as the two bantered with the intimacy of longtime friends. How I would love knowing him that well, she thought with poignant yearning.

A waitress brought a fine white wine from Ken's private stock. "It's marvelous," Katy assured him, her gaze on the waitress, who was giving Thomas a friendly smile. The wine slid like silk down her dry throat.

The music started, and it wasn't half-bad, she thought. She tried to watch the musicians, but her gaze kept coming back to Thomas. The wedge of soft dark hair exposed by his open shirt collar claimed her attention. A sudden vision of lamplight glowing on naked bronze skin sent a shiver skimming down her spine.

"More wine?" Ken asked.

Katy gave him a brilliant smile. "Please," she said. Wine helped the tension that kept seizing her throat.

Patsy, a natural chatterbox, held up the conversation. Katy jumped in now and then. Her attention kept drifting in so many different directions, she had to consciously rein it in.

When the band started playing a ballad, Thomas casually took her hand in his. The instant quickening of her pulse thoroughly disconcerted Katy. Gently she slipped her fingers free of his and curled them in her lap.

By the time they finished their drinks, she felt intoxicated, but not from the wine. Thomas sat relaxed and at ease, his hair tousled as if by a woman's hand, a languorous smile playing about his mouth. So attractive, she thought. So sexy. She was not indifferent to the appreciative feminine glances he garnered.

He caught her eye and winked. Katy felt as if she had been pierced by a fine silver dart.

Dusk was pooling under the trees when they left for the restaurant. Ordinarily in the summertime, it didn't get dark until nearly ten o'clock, but black clouds were amassing overhead.

"A storm coming," Katy predicted. She liked storms.

"It'll pass over. Feel that wind? It'll blow it straight across the sound," Thomas said.

Katy doubted it and said so. They all argued amiably as they walked to the restaurant.

The food was as delicious as Patsy claimed. Famished, Katy wasted no time polishing off her grilled salmon. Thomas's dinner was interrupted several times by people who came by their table to either shake his hand or kiss his cheek. The latter, bestowed by females, affected her with something annoyingly close to jealousy. Shaking off the emotion, she made a mental note to tighten her defenses.

The wind was blowing in hard, strong gusts when they left the restaurant and it had started to rain. Katy was tense and quiet; her long day was beginning to catch up with her. She leaned back against the seat, very much in her own space. Thomas gave his attention to the road.

The silence was beginning to feel awkward.

"Thomas, I—"

"Katy, I—"

They laughed. "You first," he said.

"I just wanted to thank you for the lovely time I had this evening," she said so primly he smiled.

"The pleasure wasn't all yours. And since you treated, I should be the one thanking you."

"You're more than welcome."

Silence again. Sighing, Katy clasped her hands and stared out the window. The rain had slackened, and stopped altogether by the time they turned onto the narrow road that led to the house.

"So much for your weather-predicting talents," she murmured.

"Well, even the real weatherman is wrong now and then. Katy, about this morning—"

"Oh, Thomas, please, let's not get into that."

"Oh, Katy, please, let's do?"

She surveyed him with wry amusement. "Do you ever listen to the word *no?*"

"Depends on the occasion." He sobered. "I'm sorry if I upset you. It wasn't intentional—God knows you've had enough distress in your life without me adding to it," he said gruffly. "I thought I could help you, and in my eagerness to do so, I came on like an insensitive jerk."

She sighed. "I'm sorry, too, for blowing up like that. I was hurt and angry and, unfortunately, that's the way I reacted."

"I hate being the cause and I don't want to upset you again. But I really do feel I can help you conquer your fear of flying. Katy, just come down to the airport with me—"

"Oh, damn it, Thomas! I can't, okay? I just can't. So give it up." She touched his hand. "Please?"

"I'm not the kind of man who gives up, Katy," he said in gentle warning.

An instant later he swore and wrenched the wheel. The ancient apple tree had fallen across the lawn. Its branches covered most of the driveway. She gasped as he slammed on the brakes. Slowly, they edged around the mountain of leaves and drove down the driveway to the garage.

"What a mess," she exclaimed as he parked the car.

Thomas agreed. He sounded preoccupied. Shivering in the night chill, Katy drew her shawl tighter and preceded him into the house.

Thomas went straight to his message machine. She walked down the hall to the bathroom. She could not make out the recorded words but she could identify voices. One was female. She waited until the messages ended before emerging again.

Thomas was in the kitchen. Jeans and a T-shirt had replaced his evening clothes, and he was shrugging on his windbreaker.

"Why don't you have a cup of herbal tea before you turn in?" he suggested, zipping up the garment. "Chamomile. It'll help you relax." He opened the door.

"You're going out?" Katy asked incredulously. The wind was wild, and thunder shook the windows.

"Yes, I have something I need to do." His lips brushed her cheek. " 'Night, Katy. Sleep well."

He walked out into the wet, black night.

Five

———

For a moment, Katy just stood there, feeling slightly stunned at his swift departure. She was immediately beset by curiosity. What sort of mission would draw him out on a night like this?

Recalling the feminine voice on the message machine, she walked around the empty kitchen, her mind running on two separate tracks.

No tea, she decided.

No speculation, either, she told herself firmly.

Tea would be soothing, though. Katy made a pot and took it to her room.

Wrapped in her sister's old pink terry-cloth bathrobe, she sat on the window seat and sipped the fragrant brew while her senses slowly became attuned to the storm-tossed night. She felt aroused by its primal glory. And needful, she admitted, a soul-deep need that sought refuge in memories. Karin had loved storms, too. They had excited her in the same kinetic way, made her come alive until she fairly glowed with energy...

But never again would Karin revel in the beauty of a storm.

Desolation clawed at Katy; its familiarity in no way weakening the grip of its talons. She had taken on the role of the protective older sister at an early age. Older by only ten minutes, she reflected, smiling. Even while their parents were alive, it had been Katy who cared for Karin.

And afterward, when they were bereft of family, it was Katy who took charge, Katy who created the security blanket of love and warmth and caring. *But I didn't take very good care of her,* she thought achingly. *She's gone and I'm still here.*

Guilt. Senseless, too unwieldy to handle, immune to logic. Tears welled up; she let them fall. According to her therapist, all facets of grief must be given full expression, right down to the cleansing anguish of final acceptance.

Downstairs, the clock struck midnight.

Feeling drained, Katy wiped her tears with the back of her hand. Unbidden, her mind drifted back to Thomas. His earnest voice, when he spoke of conquering her fear of flying, had the power to shame her. "I tried, I really tried," she whispered pleadingly.

But apparently not hard enough for him, she thought with a refreshing stab of anger.

The question she had held at bay until now suddenly surfaced. Where had he gone in that wild dark? Who was he with right now? Another woman?

None of your business, she reproved herself. The hell it isn't, a rebel part of Katy refuted. He'd been with *her* earlier tonight—didn't that make it her business?

She didn't know. She didn't even know why she *cared* so much. She'd only had one serious relationship, her failed marriage, and it was no help at all in judging this one, Katy thought moodily.

She had thought herself in love, and had even cried when the break came. But the emotions involved in her marriage felt so shallow now. The growing intensity of her feelings for Thomas was a continuing shock to her nervous system.

I haven't even known him a week! she thought with renewed anger. It seemed outrageous that he could affect her so deeply in such a short time. Like a camera lens, her mind zoomed in on the memory of how he had looked in her bedroom last night, bare-chested, pajamas riding low on his hips, hair so wonderfully tousled.

Was someone else seeing him like that? Perhaps at this very moment?

Giving in to fatigue, she went to bed, only to drift in and out of a light sleep. Deep in her heart, Katy knew she was waiting for Thomas to come home.

The luminescent dial on her bedside clock read one o'clock when Katy heard him drive in. Shortly afterward, the kitchen door opened and closed. She tensed, alert to every sound downstairs. Minutes crawled by. Her body trembled from the strain of listening so hard. Had he gone to bed? Oh, Katy! she thought despairingly.

Now he was puttering in the kitchen. Refusing to question her decision, Katy snapped on a light, jumped out of bed and pulled on her robe.

Nervous fingers combed her hair, and sashed the pink robe tightly. Stepping into the dim hallway, she hurried downstairs before she could talk herself out of it. I will not ask him where he's been, she promised herself. I will *not*.

She paused at the door and caught her breath. His hair damp and tousled, Thomas stood leaning against the counter drinking a glass of milk. His eyebrows shot up when he saw her.

Katy tightened her sash. "I got hungry," she explained.

She glanced at him, at the milk, at her hands still clenching the sash. "I'll just make some toast," she told him. "If you don't mind, that is."

"Of course I don't mind. Help yourself."

His gaze seemed to singe her skin. Acutely conscious of the electricity their closeness generated, she slipped bread into the toaster and got out Maddie's homemade apple butter.

"Looks like the storm has passed over," she remarked, to break the smoldering silence.

"Has it?"

There was a much more vital question in those two words. Katy let it pass. When she glanced at him again, she discovered hooded blue eyes fixed on her bare feet. In her haste to get downstairs, she had forgotten to put on her slippers.

Doggedly poised, she buttered the toast. His gaze followed her every move. Sizzling with awareness of her femininity, Katy took a bite, swallowed, pushed down the question that popped right back up again. "Where have you been?"

She looked appalled. Thomas grinned to himself.

"Why, were you worried about me?"

"A little, yes. It's a bad night."

"So it is." Noting her flush, he added quietly, "I went to the airport to check out wind damage. Luckily, there wasn't much."

Relief gouged her, weakening her limbs. "Oh, I hadn't thought about that," she admitted, then said quickly, "Thank goodness everything was all right." Her gaze raised to his. "I really was worried, Thomas. I—I'm so glad to see you're all right."

She was so earnest, so sweet. Thomas exhaled a breath that was half sigh, half groan. Every nerve and sinew in his body tightened as he stared at her. She was seduction itself with that glorious hair tumbling around her shoulders. The curvaceous, pink-sheathed body tantalized with its promise of endless pleasures. Her bare feet with their polished nails were so innocent and sexy he felt he might quietly go crazy if he didn't get to kiss them. He was astonished by both the object and the intensity of his desire.

Thomas had done a lot of thinking tonight, and had decided to play it cool with her. Despite their mutual attraction, it was obvious that she was trying to keep a distance between them and he respected that, as well as her reasons. But the fire blazing in his heart and body was burning away both resolve and restraint.

Katy read his intent, yet she made no move to counter it. Her own body was throbbing with excitement. She gloried in it even while she struggled against it. "Thomas, no," she said as he stepped toward her. Her denial lacked conviction even to her own ears.

Their eyes locked and she was drawn into that smoky blue gaze. In some part of her mind she despaired, knowing she was not ready for this. The rest of her reveled in his masculine demand.

"Are you sure you want me to stop, Katy?" he asked huskily, as he untied the sash of her robe and spread the edges of material apart.

He was so close his breath brushed her mouth. The voice coming from deep in his chest was pure sensuous persuasion. Katy shut her eyes, then immediately opened them. She would not hide from the answer to his question, or her own. She ached for his loving. That's why she had come downstairs.

"I don't know, Thomas," she replied, meeting his gaze again. "I truly don't know."

Thomas ran his fingers down her cheek, his blood leaping at the feel of her smooth, warm skin. The thin nightgown covering her breasts moved with each breath she took, tightening until her nipples formed sharp little peaks.

He had to force back the urge to tear open the garment that concealed her from him. *For heaven's sake, Logan!* he chastised himself. The admonition did no good. When, instinctively, he swayed toward her, her thighs and taut belly brushed against his. Passion rode him, hardening his body, coiling low and deep and demanding.

She made a sighing sound. Then her lashes fluttered down as she lifted her face to his in soft surrender.

He stilled, his body and mind clashing in tumultuous conflict. The urge to take was maddeningly strong. But there was something else there, too, something that surged into a clear, hot ache in the nether regions of his embattled self. He didn't want to just *take*. He wanted to *mate*. There was a difference, a strange, bewildering, but extremely vital difference. His hand fell from her cheek.

Her eyes flew open, two dark, hazy pools widening with confusion as he stepped back.

"I think you should know whether or not you want me to stop. After all, we are adults," he said matter-of-factly. "I want you very much. I also want the feeling to be mutual. Well, it's been a long day, so . . . goodnight, Katy." Abruptly, he walked out of the room.

Katy stood rooted to the spot, a five-foot-three-and-one-quarter-inch column of confused emotions. Finally, one surged above the others and brought a tiny smile to her lips. She knew how much Thomas desired her. She also knew he thought he could have had her. Yet he had walked away from her.

Later, lying in bed aching with unfulfilled need, Katy realized she felt amazingly good. She had trusted him enough to leave her door unlocked. And now that tight little bud of trust was blossoming into a lovely flower.

The sound of chain saws awoke Katy the next morning. Apparently Thomas had begun cleaning up the fallen apple tree, she surmised, wincing at the raucous noise. She looked at the clock with disbelief. It was after nine! Flinging her arms above her head, she indulged her body in a voluptuous stretch while her mind indulged in memory. She could still feel a trace of hunger for the kiss she had wanted so badly last night. It would have been so easy to love him. To make love to him, she hastily amended. To love him would be disastrous.

Her sister's robe lay across the rocker. Snuggling into it, Katy smiled at the warmth and comfort it gave her to wear a garment her sister had loved. Slowly, she padded to the bathroom.

A hot and cold shower made her feel tinglingly alert. She matched the morning, Katy thought whimsically. Sparkling sunlight gave everything that clean, newly washed look.

Eager to get outside, she paired a red cotton sweater with her favorite jeans, donned her sneakers, tied back her hair and swung downstairs.

She found coffee steaming in the pot. She made toast and took it out to the front porch. Thomas and three other men were cutting away at a pile of branches, their chain saws shockingly loud on the breezy air. Her gaze slid past the other males, to the one who worked shirtless, back muscles rippling as he drove an ax into a limb.

Katy bit her lip as she recalled the pinch of jealousy that had afflicted her last night. Actually more than a pinch, she conceded with a little shiver. Just imagine how it would hurt to fall in love with, and then lose, this vital man.

Straightening, Thomas wiped sweat from his forehead with a red bandanna and stuck the kerchief in his back pocket. When his gaze found hers, she lifted her cup of coffee in salute.

He sauntered over. "Hi."

"Hi, yourself." She bit into her toast, her gaze flickering to his damp, gleaming chest. He looked wonderful! "Weren't you supposed to have weekend guests?"

"They canceled because of the storm. Just as well. I doubt they'd have enjoyed this," he said, grimacing at the deafening snarl of the chain saw. His mouth curved in a quick, rueful smile. "I know you're not enjoying it, either."

"The storm's fault, not yours." Katy was quick to absolve him. Her gaze ran across his wide shoulders. The sparse hair on his chest was black and curly. She touched her tongue to her upper lip. "Flying today?" she asked brightly.

"No. Tomorrow."

"Do you have a backup pilot or something, that you can take off work when you want? Well, of course you must have," she answered her own question with a rising flush. "I mean, you can't just shut down an airline when you feel like chopping trees!"

"No, you can't do that," he agreed humorously. His blue eyes leveled to hers. "I can find some free time this afternoon if you're going to be around."

Katy knew what he meant. "I don't know if I will be or not. I haven't formed an agenda for the day yet," she said somewhat stiffly. His gaze flickered away. She wondered if he thought her a coward. "Right now I thought I'd walk through the woods that edge your meadow, take pictures of the flora and fauna," she went on with an airy laugh. "That is, if you don't mind?"

"No, of course I don't mind. I'll walk with you, in fact. There's a certain place I'd like to show you. Let me get my shirt."

Katy nodded, and went inside to fetch her camera. She checked the film, chose a different lens and slipped it into a soft leather bag, which she slung over her shoulder. She finished her coffee and toast, then went outside to wait for him.

When Thomas reappeared, she fell into step beside him. He had brought two apples, green ones with crisp white flesh and crackly skins. Munching on them, they walked through the fragrant meadow. Katy stopped now and then to gather handfuls of ripe raspberries, their taste a sweet and juicy counterpoint to the tangy apple.

"I used to walk through this meadow as a boy," Thomas mused aloud. "Used to play pirates here with Debbie, one of my sisters. We'd bury the treasure, usually some of Grandma's old necklaces. Then we'd run to the spring for drinks of cold, icy grog, which all genuine pirates drink, of course. Water, actually, but with a little imagination..."

He laughed, his skin golden in the sunlight, blue eyes sparkling between thick, dark lashes. Irresistible, Katy thought. Her heart swelled as she imagined him as a little boy running through these lush green grasses.

"Is Debbie younger than you?" she asked distractedly.

"Yeah, I'm the oldest. Debbie and Linda are married now, Susan's a doctor, with no time for marriage or babies."

"Takes after you, hmm?" Katy teased. "Do your parents still live in Baltimore?"

"Still there. Same neighborhood, same house." Thomas paused for a moment, then said, "Tell me about your sister."

"Bright and spirited. Always the adventurous one, always eager to try new things. She was so cute that being taken seriously was a problem. But when she strapped herself into the cockpit of that plane, everyone knew who was in charge."

Thomas stopped dead. "She was a pilot?"

Katy nodded.

His face sharpened. "Katy, was *she* flying that plane?"

"Yes." Puzzled, she added, "I thought I told you that."

"No, you didn't." He shook his head, dumbfounded. "How did she get into flying?"

"A twenty-first birthday present, from me." Her voice thinned. "She was hooked before she finished that first lesson. I've never seen her take to anything so fast. She was a natural, her instructor said." Katy brushed back a curl blowing across her face. "She got her own plane, began hiring out—cargo, people, she didn't care what she hauled, as long as she was up there in the sky." Shadowed violet eyes met watchful blue ones before she lowered her lashes. "I wonder, was it worth it?" she half whispered.

"Don't torture yourself like that." Thomas caught her hand and squeezed it. "But I can tell you from experience that, to a pilot, flying is a little like magic. I think part of me would die if I had to give it up."

His last remark struck Katy surprisingly hard. She discarded the rest of her apple, dropped his hand and walked on. "I guess Karin felt like that, too. She insisted people were born to fly." She gave a shaky laugh. "I'm not one of them, I've *never* been too keen about it, truth to tell."

"But you did it."

"Well, of course I did it. When necessary."

"It's not necessary now?"

"Yes, sometimes, but I—I haven't been working all that much since the accident." Katy bit her lip. "I went into a tailspin, Thomas," she blurted out. "Depression, lethargy, lack of motivation, lack of *caring,* actually. For a while I just withdrew from the world, like an animal wanting only to hide and lick its wounds."

Her chin came up and she looked him in the eye, defying him to show pity. "But I'm working on it, I'm even taking assignments again. Who knows, someday Conde Nast may just come looking for me. Well, what did you want to show me?"

The discussion was over. For now, that is, Thomas told himself. Curbing his impatience, he led her to the foot of a steep bank.

When they climbed it, Katy gasped with pleasure at the view. A glorious array of flowers streamed down the bank's opposite side. Tall pink and yellow foxgloves, dozens of them in all stages of bloom—deep blue delphiniums stabbing through like exclamation marks, red-flowered honeysuckle entwining a slender sapling. Daisies, cornflowers, cyclamen, forget-me-nots and snowy sweet alyssum tumbled around their heels.

"Breathtaking!" she murmured, positioning her camera. She snapped off photos without pause, the camera's motor an alien sound in the still bright morning. Flowers, shrubbery, Thomas. She gave equal time to all three subjects. She desperately wanted to capture the essence of this day.

Changing lenses, she swept the far vistas, turning slowly to include a glimpse of a distant island. "Just breathtaking!" she repeated to his satisfaction.

After she stopped shooting, they stood for a time enjoying the summery view.

"Surely all this didn't grow by itself," she remarked. "Who planned the garden? And who did the work?"

"I planned it. And planted it." At her surprised look, he smiled and shrugged. "It pleases me."

"I think it would please anyone," Katy said. Plagued by questions, she permitted none. Pursuing this discussion would only intensify the peculiar intimacy each word wove around them. She stole a glance at him. His shirt was unbuttoned. How she'd like to slide her hands under it, around that trim waist. And then, slowly, slowly, up his strong, muscled back...

Quickly, she stooped to pick a flower.

Thomas smiled as she tucked the white blossom behind her ear. "Katy, I'd like to ask you something," he said softly. "Something painful, perhaps, and certainly awkward, but I have a reason. You said you felt your sister's emotional sensations when the plane went down, when it burned. Is it possible you might have just imagined what she felt? Perhaps projected your own feelings into the event?''

''No! I know what I felt.''

''Empathizing with her to a great extent, yes, but also putting yourself in her place?'' he asked, despite her protest. ''Is that the basis of your fear, that you'll die as she did, if you fly again?''

''Well, of course I'm afraid of dying,'' she replied curtly. ''Most people are, Thomas. What are you, some kind of amateur shrink?''

''Oh, Katy,'' he said, spreading his hands as if in appeal. ''What if I told you there's no reason to be afraid of death?''

''Ah, you're an expert on that, too?'' She looked up at him, her mouth tilting, just the faintest curl of lip, yet Thomas felt it like a blow. He could just imagine her reaction to his near-death experience. Yet, if she believed him . . .

A big if, he reminded himself. No one else had.

Conflicted, and not as brave as he'd like to be, he replied, ''Well, maybe not an expert, but I do have firm opinions on the subject.''

''On every subject, I'd say,'' she replied. With a tight laugh, she walked back down the bank to the meadow.

Thomas chuckled and matched his strides to her steps. *Give it up, man!* logic advised. But he couldn't. It mattered too much.

''You don't like firm opinions too much, do you?'' he remarked as she paused to pick a spear of fruiting grass.

''It's not firm opinions I dislike, it's your tendency to see yourself as the final authority that rubs me the wrong way.'' She shredded the grass. ''I had enough of that from my ex-husband.''

He stilled. ''You were married?''

"Once. And yes, I loved him," she said, forestalling his question. "Idiotically so. I was so crazy about him that I..." Katy hesitated, reluctant to tell him the real reason for her divorce. It was as if her husband's infidelities demeaned her somehow. "At first, I could suppress my feelings and opinions, deny my intelligence—I even convinced myself that he was just being masterful," she said, sighing. "Anything to meet his needs. But only for a while."

"I'm not like that, and I resent the comparison, Katy," Thomas said roughly.

"No, you're not and I'm sorry if I implied you were," Katy replied, instantly contrite. What would he say if I told him how big a fool I *really* was? she wondered. "Maybe I'm a little too sensitive about it, I don't know," she said, sighing. "But he was such a domineering man. He didn't believe in equality in a relationship. Naturally someone had to have the upper hand and naturally it was him. I'm talking extremes here, Thomas. He needed to control my every action, what I thought, where I went, who I saw." Her nervous fingers plucked more berries. "After it ended, I vowed I would never subject my will to anyone else's. I don't want anything to do with controlling people, regardless of how *nicely* they do it."

"You think I'm a controller, then." He paused. "Well, maybe, a little. But authority comes naturally to any successful businessman—he *has* to take charge. And I told you I had to take care of my younger sisters, so bossing women around comes naturally, too, I guess." His hand roughed through his hair and came to rest on the back of his neck. "I'm sorry you had a bad marriage, Katy. Just don't paint me with the same brush, okay?"

She blew out a breath. "I'm going to have to work on that."

"And I'll work on the bossiness. Deal?"

"Deal!"

He took rich pleasure in capturing a wayward curl and tucking it behind her ear. "I have to go back and help those guys a while, but after that I'm free."

"To do what?"

"To take you to the airport. The plane is due in at four, and our next flight isn't until five, so, allowing time for refueling, we'll still have time to, well, just look at it, if nothing else."

Those wonderful eyes flashed. "You're very persistent, Thomas. Annoyingly so, in fact."

"I am not. I just feel very strongly about this. I know what you said and I respect it. But you need help and I want to help you."

Her chin lifted in challenge. "Has it occurred to you that I might not want your help, that I might prefer helping myself?"

"Have you been able to help yourself?"

Her color heightened. "Not altogether, no. But I told you I'm working on it," she said, gazing beyond him. "Anyway, why does it matter to you if I fly again or not? It's not your problem, it's mine."

"I'm making it mine," he said evenly. He could see in the set of her delicate jaw her determination to be independent, to make her own decisions. But he couldn't stop now. "Because it does matter to me. Because I . . . I want the pleasure of sharing the magic with you. You see, I care about you, Katy. And I protect the people I care about, it's part of my character. I care for you," he repeated, taking her hand.

The words hung in the air like drops of light.

She stared at him a moment. "Thank you, Thomas. I like you, too. But the airport . . ." She sighed. "I really don't want to do that. Please. I don't."

"You don't want to rid yourself of this phobia?"

"Yes, of course I do." Her voice rose. "But I don't want to embarrass us both in a public place!"

"There'll be no one near that plane but you and me. I wouldn't do anything to embarrass you, Katy." His voice was soft, reassuring.

She retreated behind the thick veil of her lashes. "Not you. Me. I'm afraid, Thomas," she said bleakly. "Much as I hate to admit it, I'm weak and afraid. A coward, I guess."

She shook her head and made a small, palms-up gesture of resignation. Thomas's heart clenched.

"I know you're afraid. Maybe I would be, too, in your situation," he conceded. "But I think you're a lot stronger than you give yourself credit for. And what's bravery, anyhow? Taking a chance even though you're so scared you're shaking in your boots. I know the feeling, I've had my own terrors. Please let me try to help you, Katy. Please, share my magic."

Defeated by such *gentle* persuasion, Katy thought, and gave an audible sigh. "All right, Thomas, you win. I'll go to the airport with you."

She headed for the house, her mouth set in resolve.

Silent, Thomas followed her. Words swarmed his mind, but refused to form into coherent sentences. Now that she had agreed, he was suddenly filled with misgivings about his persistence in reopening her wounds.

"More wounds than you suspected," he muttered to himself. "A bad marriage to some stupid jerk with more brawn than brains... And you're going to fix everything, right? Ri-ight."

Gnawed by self-doubt, he raked a hand through his hair. Maybe he had overestimated her strength. What if he was riding roughshod over frail defenses, defenses she desperately needed? She had a traumatic past to resolve, and if he was truly interfering in that, then he was making a huge mistake.

But he had to risk it, he told himself. Reconciling his lifestyle and her fears was important to him. He didn't know how much or in what way he cared for her, but he did know he cared. She was always in his thoughts. Thomas knew he would not be satisfied until he had won her trust.

That wouldn't be easy, given her marital fiasco. What other hurt had that bastard inflicted upon this valiant woman? he wondered savagely.

He intercepted her glance and felt his heart twist. Those lovely eyes were clouded again. He fought an urge to sweep her into his arms. *I'll keep you safe, Katy,* he vowed fiercely.

Six

The airport was located on the other side of town. During the silent drive, his misgivings increased each time Thomas glanced at her composed face. Hands clasped tightly in her lap, she stared straight ahead, unnervingly stoic. Was this truly such an ordeal for her? He simply could not relate to what she was feeling, not deep down where it counted, and he hated that.

"Katy, we're just going to look at my planes, that's all," he reminded her. "I kind of like the idea of showing them off, to be perfectly honest. Besides the two commuter planes, I have a small jet which I lease out. In fact, it's currently ferrying two corporate types and their wives to Alaska. My special love, though, is the plane I started out with, a single-engine Cessna. I've spent many an hour sky-dreaming in that baby."

"Sky-dreaming?"

He reddened. "Well, that's what I call it. When I'm flying, all my cares and troubles drop away like magic.

Who can worry about plumbing problems or bank snafus or such when you're looking at infinity? It's very peaceful," he ended lamely.

"To you, perhaps," she said, her tone neutral. "To most people, flying is just a quick way to get from here to there."

"But not to your sister."

"No, not to Karin," she conceded, turning her face to the side window.

He drew up before a long, one-story building, and they got out. Passengers milled about the small terminal. The plane the travelers were waiting on was parked behind it, boarding ramp down, ready, apparently, to take on passengers. Katy fixed her gaze on the chain-link fence enclosing the lawn as they walked toward the plane. Sweat trickled down her spine, yet she felt chilled. *It's okay,* she told herself. *You've been this far before.*

With tight control, she preceded Thomas up the ramp and stepped inside the narrow aisle. Obeying his courtly gesture, she slid into a green plush seat. "Very nice," she said. "Very comfortable." Her stomach was a clenched fist. "Could I see the cockpit?"

Looking pleased, Thomas showed her the control panel with its bewildering complexity of knobs and buttons and lights. It amazed her that he understood all this, just as it had always amazed her to watch Karin take command of her craft with such confident ease.

An extra-deep breath now and then helped conceal the trembling that afflicted her body. But she knew that his light touch was responsible for much of her composure. The strong, tanned hand he kept on her arm was warmly reassuring.

"And now let's go meet Angel," he said, escorting her down the ramp.

"Angel?"

"Uh-huh, Angel. That's what she's been to me," he replied lightly. He steered her toward an open hangar.

"Beautiful, huh?" he murmured as they stopped just inside.

Even in the dappled light of the hangar, the small plane fairly glistened. Its exterior shone with the brilliance of a polished red apple. Keeping that whimsical thought in mind, Katy approached the aircraft, trying not to acknowledge the swirl of nausea that loosened her taut stomach muscles. She heard a sudden roaring in her ears. It took several seconds to realize that the other plane was revving its engines. She swallowed, hard, fighting the sickening weakness surging through her limbs.

"It's lovely, Thomas," she said thinly.

"Not 'it,' she," he said in cheerful reproof.

He took her arm, and to her vast relief, Katy found herself being drawn out into the sunlight again. To her further relief, and a goodly dollop of surprise, she was escorted back through the terminal and out to his car without another word.

"That's it?" she asked as he got in beside her.

Thomas laughed and touched the tip of her pale, icy nose. "I said we were just going to look, Katy."

They drove back to the house in record time. Satisfied that he had accomplished a small part of his goal, Thomas was eager to get on with the tree-removing job. Most of the fallen branches were chopped up and were being wheelbarrowed to the backyard.

It was nearly noon. "If you have the fixings, I could make sandwiches for everyone," Katy suggested.

"Great! You'll find everything you need in the refrigerator. I doubt anyone would turn down a cold beer, either," he said, looking relaxed and happy as they exited the car.

He rejoined his work crew while Katy went inside to prepare lunch. She liked the idea of domesticity, she admitted. Her own heart reflected his happiness. Or maybe just relief, she mused, taking loaves of wheat and rye from the bread box. She had done what he asked—saw his planes, admired them, all without undue stress.

But that was the limit of her cooperation. Damned if she'd be pressured into anything more, she thought, slicing tomatoes with more force than was needed.

When everything was ready, she called the men inside.

Watching the ravenous men dig into the food she'd prepared gave Katy a peculiar pleasure. She joined them at the kitchen table, not really hungry, just eager to meet Thomas's friends. The gleam of masculine curiosity she caught now and then did not perturb her. Let them wonder, she thought with saucy defiance.

Later, after the wood had been stacked on the racks, the crew left, and Thomas began splitting logs for the fireplace. Katy watched for a while, fascinated by the power and accuracy each stroke of the ax displayed. He was a man who liked to work with his hands, she decided. Certainly he had the calluses to back up her conclusion. But there was more to him than this simple labor implied. Intrigued, she wondered what he had done in New York. And why had he exchanged that big-city life-style for this slow-paced rural existence? He was accustomed to being in command, to making decisions for others; look how determined he was to resolve *her* problems. What motivated the man, what made him tick?

The urgent desire to learn more about him made Katy uneasy. But when Thomas gave her the opportunity to satisfy her curiosity, she would be quick to accept it.

That evening when she asked him to recommend a restaurant, Thomas replied, "Tumbling Brook Farm. I hear it has a great chef. Oh, hush," he chided her as she began to protest. "I'm just repaying you for making lunch."

"In that case, I accept. What are we having? And can I help?" she asked—unwisely, she decided later.

Katy had no idea that preparing a meal together could create so much intimacy. The easy give and take, the closeness that they achieved without physically touching, was a stunning pleasure. Shrimp and pasta in a fresh marinara sauce, a simple tomato and lettuce salad, and hot rolls took mere minutes to prepare, and a lovely, leisurely, much longer time to consume.

The wine was red, the dusk lavender blue, the mood silken with promise. Feeling lighthearted, or maybe just light-headed, Katy amended dryly, she helped clean the kitchen, then joined him in the den for snifters of fragrant apple brandy.

She took the couch, Thomas, the chair and ottoman. Long legs outstretched, he sipped his brandy and watched her nestle into the plump cushions. After a little silence, she asked, "Do you mind if I call home, check on my housekeeper, Nell? I'll be quick."

Thomas handed her the cordless phone. Leaning back his head, he studied the ceiling while she made her call, a brief one, as promised. When she hung up, he remarked, "This Nell of yours sounds like more than a housekeeper."

"Oh yes, much more! She was our nanny when we were children. Then she married and we kind of lost touch. But four years ago, we met up again and...well, she was a widow, all alone in the world and not in the best health, so she moved in with Karin and me. She was so good to us when we were girls, so loving and protective. Which made our new living arrangements doubly wonderful, because now we could take care of her."

Katy gave a nose-wrinkling laugh. "Not that we dared let her think that's why we'd taken her in, heavens no! Anyone could see we needed a housekeeper. Busy as we were? Certainly we did! She's not senile, far from it. She's only sixty-three, and very active in the community. But I'm there if she needs me."

Thomas smiled. "I'm glad you have someone like that."

"Me, too. She's family." Katy sipped the lovely, fiery brandy. "Now I have a question for you. What did you do in New York? And why did you leave that life-style for this one?"

"I was an investor."

"A successful one?"

"Uh, you might say that." His mouth tilted in wry amusement. "I was known as the Wizard of Wall Street in certain circles," he said.

"Goodness! What, exactly, did you do?"

"I specialized in finding small companies that had major growth potential, but lacked capital. I furnished the capital, at which point it became a gamble—if I was wrong, I lost, if I was right, I won. Fortunately, I was right a lot more times than I was wrong."

"I wish I'd known you then. Maybe I would have found it easier to figure you out," she said lightly.

"You wouldn't have liked me then." His gaze leveled to hers. "I didn't much like myself then."

"Why? Have you changed so much?"

"Yes."

Katy wished he would say more. But he didn't.

She straightened her neckline. "I like you now. Why wouldn't I have liked you then?"

"I was a careless man, Katy. Careless with people, with relationships, with other people's feelings and needs."

"Careless," she repeated, lashes lowered, mouth a scornful twist. She had met one too many careless men already.

"Careless," he reinforced her easily read opinion. "Only one thing interested me during that time, what *I* felt, needed, wanted."

She sat back, her gaze almost a palpable barrier between them. "And what was that?"

"What everybody thinks they need. Money. Which translates to power. I was totally self-absorbed. It's a particularly potent form of blindness."

"But now that's all changed. Now you're a different man."

What her small, crooked smile implied made him ache. "Yes, I am."

"What changed you?" Katy asked, but then added, "If that's too personal, I withdraw the question."

"It is personal." He rose and walked to the window. "Too personal, I guess. I rarely talk about it, to anyone. Just something that happened to me, something that made me start thinking about life, purpose, the real meaning of success."

Katy waited, desperately hoping that he'd go on. "So," she said invitingly, and paused. "After you'd finished your 'thinking,' what did you do next, give away all your money?"

"No. I'm not a fool, Katy," he said dryly. "There's nothing wrong with having money. It's a wonderful tool, if you remember that's all it is, a tool, not your reason for existing."

His shrug put an end to that particular subject. "Katy, do you realize how close we've become in just these few days?" he asked abruptly.

Suddenly cautious, Katy replied, "Yes. We've become friends, I think. That is unusual—I mean, I'm not one to make friends quickly. It takes me a while to, well, to trust someone that much, I guess."

"I think we've become friends, too," he agreed. "I also think I could fall in love with you."

Katy came to her feet, trying to take a breath of suddenly nonexistent air, shaking her head in swift denial. "No! Don't say that, Thomas, please don't. Let's stay friends. Friends don't hurt each other. And that's what would happen if we...this would lead *nowhere*. Believe me, I know what I'm saying. Falling in love with me would be a big mistake, a total waste!''

Clearly taken aback by her vehemence, Thomas stared at her. ''Love is never wasted,'' he refuted with intensity. ''But I would like to know why you think so.''

Nettled, and fighting a throat-tightening sense of desolation, she said, ''You should be able to guess why.''

''Because your sister was a pilot and died in a plane crash?''

It sounded so stark the way he said it. Katy sat down and crossed her legs. ''Yes, all right, that's part of it, but my reasons are far more complex than that.''

''I know that. I just wanted to make sure you did. And I need to hear those reasons, Katy. You're mixed up and hurting and I need to know exactly why. Not for curiosity's sake, but because I want so much to understand you. Do you believe me?''

She nodded. ''It's just so hard to talk about certain things. Like my marriage, for example,'' she said with a small, knowing smile. ''That is what you need to know about, isn't it?''

''Part of it.'' Thomas shifted position. ''What did he do for a living?''

''He was, and still is, an actor. Quite a good one, too.'' Her voice grew even dryer. ''*I* believed him. His real name's Ryland Dixon.''

Katy stood up and jammed her hands into her pants pockets. ''On screen, he's known as Rhys Dillion. He believes that has more cachet. He's not a household name yet, but he intends to be. What more do you wish to know about that 'handsome, sexy, every woman's fantasy,' to quote his latest press release? That he ran out on me? True enough. You want to know why? Or at least the reasons he gave me? I wasn't *fun* enough. And I refused to play his version of musical beds."

"Musical beds?" he queried softly. "He was unfaithful?"

"Yes. I know I sound flippant, but talking to you like this is very difficult. It's so deeply personal," she said, sighing.

She paced to the window. "He said I had to share the blame for his lapses, that I'd failed him, too. I didn't challenge him enough, he said. Well, I guess that's true— I *was* too provincial to play the games people play. So he found another player. We didn't even make it to our first anniversary."

"That must have been rough," Thomas said.

"Well..." She shrugged, then suddenly wheeled around to face him. "No, I refuse to shrug it off," she said fiercely. "It's an important part of my past, damn it. Because it *changed* me and anything that changes a person that much *matters!* His infidelity and controlling personality hurt, but it also diminished me and left me feeling less than I was. He destroyed the hopes and dreams I'd brought into my marriage. And in the process, he destroyed my innocence."

"You're absolutely right," Thomas mused aloud. "I've never thought of it like that, but you're right. I guess it would feel that way. Must have left some pretty deep scars."

"Nothing wrong with scars, they're visible proof of lessons learned," she said shortly. Sitting down again, she gave him a rueful look. "Sorry, I didn't mean to snap at you. But I'm not a poor waif in dire need of rescue, Thomas. I'm quite capable of helping myself. And I will."

"I know you will, eventually. I'd just like, very much, to assist you. And maybe speed up the process a little."

She sipped her brandy. "You don't know me, Thomas, and I certainly don't know you, and don't you say I do," she warned. "I'm not into fantasy."

"Mmm," he murmured, but let her statement pass. Rising, he refilled their glasses. "So what don't you know about me? That's important, I mean."

She eyed the lean, powerful figure coming toward her. "Well, well, everything, damn it. I don't know how you think, how you feel... Heavens!" she said, forcing a laugh. "We're probably poles apart in our opinions of—of just about everything."

"Like what? Give me an example."

"Well, just the basics, love, commitment, marriage." She paused, then said, "What's your idea of the perfect mate? Or are you even the marrying kind?"

"The perfect mate?" Looking thoughtful, he walked back to his chair and settled himself again. "Let's see, what do I want? A gorgeous, sexy, lusty woman, to begin with. With desirable character traits, of course—integrity, honesty, trustworthiness, patience... Someone who's tenderhearted, sweet-natured, a woman who has a great sense of humor."

"Good grief," Katy muttered. "Does such a paragon actually exist?"

Twinkling blue eyes raised to her face. "One can hope. Let's see, what else do I want in a mate? She'd be a homebody, content to keep my house, warm my bed, raise my kids, wash my socks and be here to welcome me home every evening with hot kisses and a hot meal."

"Dream on, Thomas!" Katy said with a gusty laugh. "That does let me out, though. I hate housework, I rarely cook and I haven't decided about having kids yet. I fully intend to keep on working as long as I can. Which means traveling, spur-of-the-moment trips hither and yon..." She raised her hands, palms up. "So I was right. We *are* poles apart. Irreconcilable differences."

His laugh was low and easy. "Irreconcilable, Katy?" Rising, he drew her up, too, and slid his hands up her arms. "Do you really think so?"

"Don't be smug, Thomas," she said, breaking free.

"I'm not being smug, just pretty sure you want me as much as I want you. Am I wrong?"

"No. Satisfied?" she challenged.

"Not by a long shot." Thomas claimed her mouth before she could utter—or even think about uttering—a protest.

It was a deep, thorough, soul-searing kiss, one that drew them together into a single silhouette. Katy didn't know at what point she stepped into his embrace, wasn't specifically aware of the moment her arms lifted and wound around his neck. It was such a natural sequence of events, culminating with her lips opening to his tongue, her breasts burning into his chest, her body seeking and finding the hard male strength of his.

Thomas dragged his lips from the hot sweetness of her mouth to the heated silk of her neck. Her scent wove its own magic spell around him. The sensuous drum of his heartbeat echoed the pulse beating wildly at the base of her throat. He was intensely aware of her, all of her, from the softness of her hair to the feminine roundness of her breasts and hips, the tender plane of her belly, the strength of her supple limbs. And her eyes, he thought, feeling a little unsteady as he lifted his head to meet her gaze, those enchanting violet eyes. He felt incredibly strong and incredibly weak. With a low groan, he laid his forehead against hers.

"We would be so good together, Katy, so very good."

"I have no doubt of that, Thomas Logan," Katy said breathlessly. "I'm sure you'd be good with any woman."

"No. That's not what I meant. And I think you know it, I think that last remark was just a smoke screen."

"Maybe it was, but I needed it." Her laugh was throaty. "If you can make me feel like this with just a kiss, what would making love be like?"

"Mmm, maybe we'd both go up in flames." He nibbled her earlobe. "But I'm willing to chance it. Are you?"

She drew back and looked up at him to ask, "Do you realize I haven't even been here a week? One week, Thomas. And we're having this intimate conversation after only five days—am I the only one who finds that a bit strange?" she asked, defying his tender, knowing smile. "I mean, it really *is* incredible."

"With anyone else, yes. With you, no. Kismet? Karma? Destiny? I think so. But right now, the only thing I care about is waking up in the morning and finding you still here." Thomas tipped up her chin. "I give you fair warning, Katy Lawrence—I intend to do everything in my power to ensure that."

Before she could come up with a response that made sense, he caught her hand and turned toward the front door. "It's a great night. Let's go sit on the swing and look at the moon and talk."

"Oh, but I-I'm really quite tired . . ." She sighed. *And wanting, needful* . . . "What things?"

"I'd like to discuss in more detail what it would be like to make love . . ."

Katy awoke to the bright new morning with a sense of wary wonder. When she went to bed last night, she'd thought she would toss and turn and analyze and agonize until dawn. She simply wouldn't sleep a wink. Instead, she had snuggled down under the luxurious comforter, tried to organize her thoughts and tumbled into deep, sound slumber.

This morning, the memory of last night lay upon her mind like dew on summer grass, sweet and clinging, impossible to ignore. Mentally, she censored the kiss and hurried on to Thomas's warning statement, which had shocked, thrilled and very nearly rendered her mute, she admitted. Then he had taken her hand and practically towed her out to the moonlit veranda. And then? Then they'd talked. Of what it would be like to make love, as he had said, and other things, too.

Nothing important, just ordinary things. Oh, but the talk had been so easy! She had felt like a girl again, wanting to run away to safety, wanting just as much to stay and sample the dangerous delights he offered.

Her breath caught as she remembered what else he had said last night. *I want you here in the morning. I intend to do everything in my power to ensure that.* The words flowed together to form an incandescent bracelet for her heart.

She shivered suddenly, thinking of another radiant morning, a California morning, all golden sunlight and bird song—and the huge, orange fireball glowing against the blue, blue sky.

Without warning, a deep inner gate opened and anguish poured over her in icy torrents. "Oh, Karin, I miss you," she cried. "I miss you so much! Oh, God, what I'd give to hear your voice again." Tears rained down her cheeks. She let them fall. "Sometimes I feel so needful, Karin," she whispered, covering her face with her hands.

Bitterly she wept.

Something, a wisp of thought, perhaps, brought her head up. "I can't let him get close, I can't, I just can't. There's too much pain in loving, too much hurt in caring. I can't take any more hurt. Damn it, I've lost too many people already!" she declared.

But her heart beat out its own insistent message, and it was telling her to trust Thomas. She pulled on a robe and headed for the bathroom.

After a quick shower, she dressed in jeans, cotton shirt and sturdy sneakers. Makeup camouflaged her reddened eyes and nose. She found her baseball cap and placed it firmly on her head. Camera and denim jacket in hand, she went downstairs and strode to the kitchen.

Thomas stood in front of the window, sipping coffee. His expression, in profile, was pensive, a moodiness that communicated itself to Katy even before he turned to greet her.

"'Morning, Katy."

"'Morning, Thomas." His hair was still damp and curly from his shower. She cleared her throat. "Why are you up so early?"

"I knew you'd be up early."

Katy set down her camera bag. "Are you now psychic?"

"I wish I were. Hungry?"

"Yes." Katy glanced at the beautiful fruit salads he had arranged on two white plates—raspberries, red and gold, scarlet strawberries and slices of pale green melon, all on crisp, dark green sprigs of mint.

"Those look delectable, Thomas. Almost too pretty to mess up, in fact. You an artist, too?"

He smiled, appreciating her insouciant air. "Not quite. Maddie made this yesterday. Please, sit down. Coffee?" He filled her cup and sat down across from her. "Where are you running off to this morning?"

"I'm not running off, I have a job to do and I'm going to do it." Katy lightened her tone. "Mount Constitution, for starters, then onto the ferry for a little island-hopping."

He picked up his fork. "Can you make a living writing for magazines?"

"Sure, if you give up a few things like food and clothing. Lucky for me I don't have to depend on my paycheck for such luxuries."

"Ah. Divorce settlement?"

"Trust fund," she corrected, annoyed at his assumptions.

Thomas's rueful smile sufficed for an apology. They sipped coffee. He watched her over the rim of his cup. Finally, he said, "Katy, I can tell that you have something to say, so say it."

"Yes, I do." Katy cleared her throat again. "I'm going to spend this weekend out on my own . . . away from you, to be more accurate."

His face impassive, Thomas said, "I've made you feel uneasy about being around me."

"Well, yes, there is a certain awkwardness. It's too much too soon, Thomas. Just too fast for my tastes. It's not my nature to rush into things. I, well, damn it all, I'm a woman who thinks with her head, not a girl who . . ." Her mouth quirked. "Who flies by the seat of her panties, so to speak."

His fine mouth mimicked hers. "So to speak. I have to be honest with you—I relived that kiss over and over last night. But I'm sorry, Katy, sorry I came on so strong. It's a habit I've developed of late. I'm not a particularly fearful person, so I forget that others are, and how very strong fear can be."

She half frowned, half scowled. "You're not afraid? At all?" Her nose wrinkled. "How did you accomplish *that* particular feat?"

"I didn't say I wasn't afraid, I said I wasn't particularly fearful. Not usually, at any rate. However, I find *you* quite terrifying."

A spark of devilment flashed in his eyes. Katy sniffed. "So how did you? Stop being so fearful, I mean."

"Comes with the territory."

His oblique response piqued her interest, but he'd already risen to bring two bowls of hot, buttered oatmeal to the table. Toast followed. "Eat," he said. "You're too thin."

"That'll be the day." She poked a spoon into the oatmeal. "Nell always insisted we eat our oatmeal. I loved it, but Karin hated it. So I always switched my empty bowl for her full one. Kept her out of trouble."

Her lashes fanned up. "I've been considering moving to the Rosario Resort."

"That's ridiculous, you don't—" He broke off as she arched an eyebrow. "All right, maybe not ridiculous, but damn it, you don't have to go to such lengths, at least not on account of me."

"I feel I do, Thomas," she told him. "I'm still mourning my sister, still healing from a wounding relationship. I'm just not ready for..." Her lips quirked. "For a ride to the moon."

"Grief is its own master," he acknowledged. "But you can heal yourself, Katy. Okay, okay, I'm backing off!" he said as her eyes flashed. "In fact, I have some overnight charters this weekend, so I'll be in and out. Maddie stays here when I'm out if I have guests. So you won't be alone, in case that's a problem."

"I have no problem with being alone." She arched an eyebrow. "Unless you're afraid I'll walk off with some of your valuables?"

"No. I trust you with my valuables. In fact, I'd trust you with my life," he said lightly. "So you'll stay on?"

She nodded, smiling faintly.

"I'll cancel Maddie, then." He stood up and reached for his jacket. "I'm glad you're staying on here. Have fun on your explorations, there really is a lot to see. Lopez isn't much on tourism, being generally a private development, but San Juan Island is worth your while. Oh, and when you get to Friday Harbor, check out the Nina Logan Youth Center. I think you'll enjoy seeing what an effective tool money can be when it's used right." He raised his hand. "Ciao," he said, and sauntered out of the room.

He was at the front door when her tart query caught up with him. "Do you *always* have to have the last word?"

His laugh rumbled up from deep inside his chest as he walked out into the lambent morning. She would be there when he returned, and that's all that mattered right now.

Seven

"Katy, haven't we gone far enough?" Patsy groaned. "I know you've climbed trees, braved white-water rapids and forded crocodile-infested rivers, all for the sake of that perfect picture, but must we scale this entire mountain?" she asked. "I grant you the thrill of victory, but what about the agony of 'de feet'? Mine are killing me!"

"Oh, stop griping, Patsy, you said you wanted to come hiking with me, so here we are," Katy scolded, but her voice was soft and her smile pensive. "Okay, I guess we've gone far enough. Here's a nice, comfy rock. Let's rest a while."

"Thank heaven for small favors!" Patsy sat down on the wide, flat rock and took off a sneaker to shake it out. "So, Katy. Why so subdued this morning? And don't go all innocent on me—I know good and well you're uptight about something."

Katy stared off into the distance. "Maybe you don't recall, but we made a pact in college not to 'fix' each other up."

"Yeah, I remember." Patsy squinted at her. "So?"

"So I feel you set me up with Thomas."

"That's not what you're uptight about," Patsy said. "What's really bothering you? Why so down?"

Katy released an audible breath and sank onto the other side of the rock. "Because last night was so wonderful it makes my heart ache," she said simply.

"Aha!"

"Aha nothing. We merely sat on the veranda until the wee hours talking. But it was so... *beguiling* to do that common, ordinary thing." She lifted her hair off her neck. "So, Patsy, why was your 'aha' so joyous?"

"Because I like him and I love you."

"And one and one always makes two," Katy said. She sighed heavily. "Look, Pat, I know you meant well, that's why I'm not flying off the handle."

"You're not? Could have fooled me."

"You've obviously forgotten what I'm like when I am flying off the handle," Katy said, but her friend's droll wit was disarming. Brushing her fingertips across the carpet of tiny pink and white wildflowers, she glanced at Patsy's open face. "Oh, honey, I know you wouldn't do anything to hurt me, you're my best friend. But Pat, the man's a stranger. A charming stranger, but still a stranger. In a way, you're asking me to put my trust in someone I don't even know."

"*I* know him."

"All right, I accept that. But he's also a pilot. Patsy, he flies around in that little coffin of a plane—"

"That's a very nice plane. I've been up in it."

"Oh, Patsy! You know what I mean!"

"Yes, I do, and I respect your feelings. But if you could just let yourself trust him enough to, well, to let him try to prove you wrong about flying, maybe you'd change your mind about him, too. I bet that's why he's so eager to help you."

Sighing at Katy's uncooperative silence, Patsy put on her shoe and took off the other one. "Okay, so I set you up with him, so sue me for meddling. And if I'm really wrong, I apologize."

Katy fixed her gaze on the indistinct outline of the Cascades looming like darker clouds in the thick haze that veiled their peaks. "You're not all wrong, Patsy. I find Thomas Logan extremely appealing. But I fooled myself once before, you know? Just out and out deceived myself because I *wanted*. So I took what I wanted, grabbed it like a greedy child. I've learned not to grab, and I've learned to avoid self-deception like the plague. I'd be fooling myself if I didn't admit I'm confused and skeptical about him. Well." She shook herself. "That's all I wanted to say. I love your reason for meddling, but please stop meddling. Now stretch out your legs, tilt your head and say cheese. You're going to be a model, Patsy."

The house was empty when Katy returned late that evening. Signs of the maid's presence were evident in Katy's clean room and the stack of neatly folded towels on the dresser, but apparently Maddie had already gone home for the day.

Katy didn't mind. The big house was warm and friendly, and filled with what her California friends would have referred to as "good vibes." She stripped off her clothes. Lord, she felt grungy! Her muscles were sore from all that walking, exploring stony beaches and lonely little coves. A good long soak in the hot tub would be blissful. There was one on the rear deck, all private and cozy in its shelter of vines and ferns. If it was still heated . . .

It was. Sinking up to her neck in its heavenly depths, Katy relaxed her nude body and drifted. Although she had kept focused on her work today, she'd also done a lot of thinking. But she felt too good to probe and analyze tonight. Whatever conclusions she came to would surface in their own good time, she thought languorously.

That night she slept well, a healing process in its own right, Katy decided as she prepared her breakfast the next morning. She hadn't dreamed, hadn't been jerked awake by nightmares. She was hungry, and was eager to start the day. It was a long time since she'd experienced these simple, basic needs, and they blended in with the glory of the morning.

Even her anxiety about being so happy had a softer edge.

For a time, she sat in Thomas's chair in the living room, sipping coffee, enjoying the homey sounds of the house. Its smell swept her back to her childhood, hurtfully poignant, yet so very sweet with warm, fuzzy memories of evenings spent with Grammy and Karin in another time, another place.

Later, dressed in a pair of jeans and a sleeveless sweater, she walked through the dewy meadow collecting wildflowers for a bouquet for her room. Lord, she thought, when was the last time I picked a wildflower bouquet! That time Karin and I took that little cabin in the Catskills for a week. We had flowers all over the place. We sure made a memory that week.

Humming to herself, Katy returned to the house and arranged the flowers. She had gathered enough to share, so she made a small bouquet for Thomas and placed it on the table beside his chair.

By ten she was on the ferry to San Juan Island. For hours she wandered around Friday Harbor jotting down notes, taking pictures, working her way to the Nina Logan Youth Center.

A rambling structure that had been added on to with charming disregard for symmetry, at first glance, the cen-

ter masqueraded as an estate. It was set well back from the
street in a grove of trees. The reason for its isolation became apparent when Katy entered the front yard. Children of all ages gamboled in its beautifully equipped
playground. Inside the double front doors, teenagers
reigned: in the lobby, in the gym with its gleaming wooden
floor and basketball hoops, in the bedrooms crammed
with bunks, cots, sofa beds and anything else someone
needing a place to stay could use. Katy made notes here,
too, more for Thomas than for her assignment.

It was nearly seven when she returned home. To Tumbling Brook Farm, Katy corrected herself. A sense of keen
anticipation rode with her, increasing as she drove up the
lane and parked in front of the old white house.

No one was there to greet her. Not the one she wanted,
at any rate, Katy admitted as she tossed a quick hello to
Maddie, who was on her way out.

In the silence a clock ticked loudly. Setting down her
camera case, Katy peered into the living room. He had
been home at some point; newspapers lay beside his chair.
But he wasn't here now. Biting her lip against the surprisingly strong sting of disappointment, she went upstairs,
opened her laptop computer and transcribed her notes.
Afterward, feeling a touch of melancholy, she nestled
down on the windowsill.

It had been two days since she had seen Thomas. I miss
him, she admitted, hugging her knees. I miss him very
much.

Although she disliked knowing she was waiting for him,
she had to admit that, too. She wanted to see him. She
needed to be kissed breathless, she needed his arms around
her, hard and strong and loving. Her need existed of itself, a force that was impervious to either logic or self-
discipline.

Dusk gathered, and soon the night settled in around
Tumbling Brook Farm. She wasn't afraid of being alone;

the house wrapped her in its own peculiar security blanket. She was just a little lonely, that's all.

She phoned Nell, and after a cozy chat with her, she went to bed. Eventually, she fell asleep, still waiting.

Friday evening Thomas drove swiftly up his lane. It was late and he was tired. Too tired to feel this damn good, he thought wryly. But the lights were on in his house and the porch light shed its golden radiance to guide his steps. The sight of her car parked in its rightful place put wings on his heels. He had not seen her for more than a week and he felt as hungry and thirsty for her presence as for food and drink after a long fast.

It had been difficult staying away. True, he had the charters to occupy him, but he could have returned before tonight. But he had promised. *Give her time,* he reminded himself when his needful ache had threatened to gain the upper hand.

He had warned himself to cool it, back off, revert to the sophisticated man he knew himself to be. These adolescent feelings were rather embarrassing, to be honest. So resolved, he stepped into the house.

She was in the living room curled in his chair in front of the fireplace. She was wearing jeans and a white, man-tailored shirt, her hair in a ponytail and big red-framed glasses perched on her shiny nose.

His heart was going crazy.

"Hi, Thomas," she said with an airy wave.

"Hi, yourself." She was barefoot and he caught the sparkle of a dainty ankle bracelet. Feeling light-headed, he tossed his jacket over a chair. It had begun raining earlier and he was damp and chilled. On the outside. Inside, bonfires raged.

She removed her glasses and absently polished the lenses with the tail of her shirt. "It was so cool I built a fire, although not too well. Maybe you can fix it for me. Oh, and I have the kettle on if you'd like to join me for hot tea."

"Yes, of course, a fire. And hot tea sounds great." Thomas gave himself a shake. A rainy evening, Katy and a fire—God, he hadn't dared hope for such a wonderful end to a very miserable day.

And later? Love had to come later, it *had* to. Katy went to the kitchen. He walked over to the fireplace and began building her a real fire, taking enormous pleasure in the small task.

She padded back into the room with a laden tray. Fragrant steam curled from the teapot. Placing the tray on the coffee table, she nestled into the couch and tucked her bare feet under her. Thomas poked the fire until he was satisfied with the flames crackling around aromatic applewood.

"That's a wonderful fire!" Katy exclaimed, hugging herself. The afghan he promptly spread over her legs chased away the chill and left her feeling toasty, comfortable and cared for.

It was a lovely way to feel. And dangerous, she reminded herself as he settled down beside her. Shifting away from him, she poured their tea and slanted an eyebrow in question.

"Two lumps," he said.

Gracefully she picked up the tongs and sugared his tea, then passed his cup before preparing her own.

"Well, how did your week go?" he asked.

She told him, then asked him the same question, and listened attentively while he told her about his week. They looked at each other—and burst out laughing.

The tension between them shattered. Boneless with delight, she sat back, cup in hand, very much in her own space.

The fire crackled and the rain came down in harmonious accord. Seduced by her sense of well-being, she murmured, "This is such a lovely room, Thomas. Lovely house, for that matter."

"You like my house?"

"Oh, yes, I really do. The first time I saw it I felt such a strong sense of déjà vu," she said dreamily. "And then when I walked inside, it got downright spooky!"

She laughed, suddenly embarrassed. "Not that I'm superstitious. Well, maybe I am, a little, but everything in here looked so, well, just like it should look. It was perfect. Then I realized that it reminded me of my grandmother's house. Not necessarily the furnishings or anything like that, although she did have lace curtains and wood floors. But it was the aura that touched me, the patina of love and laughter and tears that old, beloved houses take on."

She grimaced. "Am I making any sense?"

"Very much." He set his teacup aside and shifted to face her. "When I acquired this place," he told her, "my grandparents took only a few select pieces of furniture. So I found myself with a houseful of stuff I didn't even think I wanted."

Her mouth curved enchantingly. He cleared his throat, feeling the hot beat of desire cannoning through his body.

"But then, walking around these rooms with some vague idea of turning them into a chrome-and-leather bachelor's pad like the one I'd had in New York, I began feeling the same way you do—the house was perfect just as it was."

"Good for you." She set her teacup beside his. "Mmm," she murmured with a luxurious stretch, "this is so nice."

Her eyes were half-closed, her face upturned. She was warm, close, captivating.

Thomas's response was totally logical, at least to his embattled body. He simply stood up, pulled her to her feet and kissed her with all the passion his heart and soul could hold.

Katy knew a moment of sweet, wild panic. Then, as if with a will of their own, her lips softened, and opened in sensual welcome. Her hands slid over his shoulders, moving with silken fingertip caresses up his neck and into his hair. Erotic pleasure held her there, tight against him, heartbeat to swift, pounding heartbeat.

When they came up for air, Katy gazed intently at his taut face, memorizing the clean, well-defined line of his jaw, the purposeful set of his mouth, the blue eyes dark with the desire she felt in his body. Under her scrutiny his face changed, the corners of his mouth lifting, his eyes crinkling with his smile. Her indrawn breath was nearly a gasp. She felt something let go inside her, leaving her body fluidly loose and at ease.

And leaving her at war with herself, Katy acknowledged. The desire swirling through her body was so lovely, so deliciously warming. She should struggle against that drugging warmth. But she didn't want to struggle, didn't want to fight the excitement ignited by his closeness. She wanted to throw caution to the winds, be bold and daring. With a sudden sense of triumph, she wound her arms around his neck and leaned back in his embrace.

"My sister and I used to do something we called making a memory," she said. "It didn't matter what the memory was, a vacation, a trip to the park, a nude dip in some remote lake, whatever. It didn't matter. It was just something that we'd never forget, something that would stay with us for always." Her gaze lowered to his mouth, her smile soft, sensuous. "Let's make a memory, Thomas."

Thomas drew a hard breath. "That's all I'd be to you, just a memory of some very good sex?" he asked roughly.

"No, of course not, I didn't mean that at all!" She flattened her palms against his chest, her gaze hurt and angry. "I just shared something very special with you, something very dear to me!"

"I know you did, and I appreciate that. But I don't want to make a memory with you, I want to make love with you."

He drew her into his arms once more. "I don't know where this is going to lead and right now I don't care. I just want to love you. Like this... and this..." His mouth traced a pattern of hot little kisses over her face. Her head fell back and the kisses continued down her neck to the open collar of her shirt.

When he murmured her name, her lashes slowly fanned up to reveal passion-filled violet eyes. She smiled. Without another word, Thomas swept her up in his arms and carried her to his bedroom.

She made a sound halfway between a gasp and an excited little laugh, and splashed kisses all over his face. Loving the way she felt in his arms, Thomas let her slide down his body until her bare feet touched the carpet.

Quickly, he switched on the lamp. Slowly, savoring the moment, he drew her shirt over her head. She wore nothing beneath. He dropped the garment onto the floor, pulled off the scarf that held her ponytail and loosened her hair. It fell in curling drifts around her bare shoulders. She looked up at him, her eyes deep, dark, shining. He experienced a twofold urge to protect and dominate. Groaning, he cupped her breasts, then lowered his head to take the rosy little nipples in his mouth.

Katy swayed as her knees weakened under the tender onslaught of his lips and teeth. Her mind whirled; she couldn't think, didn't want to think. She kissed the top of his bent head. Her pulse throbbed with a kind of primitive music singing in her blood until she shuddered with it.

Thomas felt the lovely shiver racing through her soft flesh. He thrust his hands into the tangled glory of her hair and drew her face to his with an extraordinary blend of roughness and tenderness.

Katy met his kiss with fiery ardor. His mouth was firm and masterful. His body, taut with anticipation, excited her and brought her deeper into his embrace. She gasped his name and clung to him, lost, wonderfully lost, in the magic they created together.

Drawing back in a blaze of reluctance and eagerness, he undressed, laughing as she hastened to help him, until they fell across the bed in a tangle of arms and legs and kisses.

Katy felt his gaze sweep over her with visceral pleasure. It burned the skin of her throat, her breasts, her belly and the contour of slender thighs and legs. "You are lovely," he said huskily. "Every inch of you, pure loveliness."

"So are you," she murmured. She traced his hard, sculpted lines with dancing fingers. "Beautiful."

He laughed and showered her with indiscriminate kisses. In the soft light, he looked at, tasted and explored her body with pagan delight.

Urgency clawed at him. There was no awkwardness as he came to her, no unease. Only joy, wonder, fulfillment.

For the first time in his life, Thomas knew the meaning of two people becoming one flesh.

And it awed him.

Katy yawned luxuriously. The room was dark now. She had no idea how much time had passed and didn't really care. She was wonderfully tired, sated with lovemaking, every muscle, bone and cell divinely relaxed.

Beside her, Thomas stirred lazily. "Think I'll sleep in tomorrow," he said with a prodigious yawn. "Usually I get up at five or so to work in my gardens."

"You do? You're like a puzzle continually unfolding," she said softly.

"Just a simple man, doing the best he can," he intoned, making her laugh. He kissed her shoulder, marveling at the smoothness of her skin. "Shall I open the drapes and let the moonlight in?"

"Oh, yes. And open the window, too."

"The window's already open. Don't go away, I'll be right back." Chuckling at her muffled response, he slid out of bed.

When he drew the drapes, the night air romped in like a boisterous spirit, weaving the scent of flowers into the delicious perfume of love. It made goose bumps rise on his skin. He returned to bed and drew her close again.

The contrast of cool air and snuggly comforter delighted Katy's senses. "Mmm, this is wonderful," she murmured.

"Yes it is. Keep that in mind, okay?"

"I will. I will also keep in mind that old saying—if it seems too good to be true, it usually is."

"Cynic," he accused, nuzzling her.

"No, just a realist. I'm only trying to keep my eyes open. No hostage to fortune, I," she said drowsily.

"Katy, hush up and go to sleep."

"I can't."

"Why not?"

"I can't sleep all scrunched up against someone."

"Thank God! Neither can I." Scooting over, he laid a hand on her arm. "How's this?"

"Good. This is good. I've never been able to sleep all wrapped up." She yawned. "Well, that's not quite true. When we were little, Karin used to leave her bed and crawl into mine and we'd sleep wrapped in each other's arms. But everything was so scary back then. Mutual protection against things that go bump in the night, I guess."

"You make me ache with stories like that," he said, sighing. "I had a wonderful family. I didn't know it, of course. I was much too busy accomplishing whatever goal

I'd set for myself. Sometimes I wonder how people put up
with me." He laughed. "Especially my sisters. I ap-
pointed myself their guardian whether they wanted a
guardian or not."

"Having been a girl, I doubt they did!" she agreed.
"Oh, I stopped by the Nina Logan Youth Center today.
Thomas, that's a magnificent thing for you to do."

"Thank you," he returned with a peculiar gruffness.

For a while longer, their murmuring voices drifted out
into the night to blend with the wind. Eventually the soft,
intimate sounds sighed away. Sweetly, they slept.

To Katy's surprise, awakening to find herself in Thomas's bed did not startle her in the least. But it did make her
feel a little uneasy. Things were so much clearer in the
bright morning light. I shouldn't be here, she thought. But
that admonition didn't have much effect on her. She felt
so *good*. With a voluptuous stretch she worked out the
kinks in various muscles.

Thomas's side of the bed was empty. But his dusky scent
was on his pillow. Clutching it to her chest, she looked
around with feminine enjoyment. She hadn't really seen his
bedroom last night. This huge bed looked new, but the rest
of the furnishings looked as if they had been cared for
lovingly and long.

The down comforter was white, as were the carpet,
draperies and cushy leather chair. Even the roses on his
bureau were white. The walls, however, were a soft, se-
rene blue. The only other spots of color came from brass
lamps and the bookshelves framing the white brick fireplace.

Slowly, reluctantly, she left the warmth of the bed. In the
alcove sitting area she discovered a small round table filled
with framed family portraits. Thomas had a handsome
family, she thought as she surveyed the display, her throat
crowding with poignant envy.

Where was he? Suddenly anxious to know, she hurried to the bathroom. To her surprise, her pink robe hung alongside his on the back of the door. She put it on, finger-combed her hair, and went in search of him.

He was in the kitchen, juicing oranges. Feeling shy and uncertain, she paused in the doorway. "Hi," she said.

"Good morning, Katy," he said, his voice soft, deep and husky enough to send shivers through her from head to toe. "Sleep well?"

She cleared her throat. "Yes, very well." She stared at him searchingly. Did he have any doubts about last night, any regrets? Her heart fluttered like a wild thing.

"I'm finding this a little difficult," she confessed. "Awkward, I guess. Do you feel that way too? No, I guess not. Men don't."

"Men do." He wiped his hands on a clean cloth. "Sometimes, when it's important. My own particular difficulty is stopping myself from slipping you between two slices of bread and having you for breakfast. You look delicious."

Her lips twitched. "Yeah, I bet. I was in such a hurry to find you I didn't even wash my face. You been up long?"

"Not long. And your face is lovely. Exquisite, in fact." He crossed the room and kissed her forehead, nose and lips. "I like your pink robe," he declared.

"Thank you. It's Karin's . . . was Karin's."

He had no fitting response, so he hugged her for a comforting moment. "I thought, if you'd like, we'll drink our juice, great big glasses of it, fresh squeezed," he said, gesturing to the empty orange halves on the counter. "Then we'll drive to a place I know and walk for an hour or so, then have breakfast at the bakery. After that, there are any number of places I want to show you. It's just a matter of choosing one. You game?"

"I'm game," Katy said. "On one condition. No pressure, no serious talk. This is all a little scary, to be frank.

I'm not much good at it. This morning-after stuff, I mean."

He laughed and squeezed her slim shoulders. "I find it a little terrifying myself. Okay, no pressure, no serious talk. Just getting to know each other."

"Agreed. Okay, I'll go shower."

Thomas deliberated for an entire second. "I'll help you," he decided.

Their walk through the crisp, clean air of the forest was invigorating. Katy was famished by the time they reached the fragrant little bakery introduced to her by Patsy.

Thomas ordered croissants and gourmet coffee for two, and Katy dug in with unabashed pleasure. Looking up to catch him smiling at her, she swallowed and asked, "What?"

"The way you eat, so precise and elegant. I love it!"

"Grammy Rose's teaching—anything you do, do it with elegance. From Miss Pickle, our fourth grade teacher, we learned how to curtsy and how to set a formal table. Her name was actually Perkins, but Pickle fit her expression much better, we thought."

"Is that the royal 'we' or are you referring to the entire class?" Thomas asked, watching her over the rim of his cup.

Her color rose. "I meant Karin and me, as you well know."

Thomas let it pass, hoping he had made his point about the symbiotic relationship she'd apparently had with her sister. And possibly still had, though she appeared unaware of it. He ordered two cups of coffee to go, and they got back in the car.

They passed small farms, through green fields vibrant with wildflowers and white-faced cattle. Now and then, rounding a curve, they caught glimpses of the sound's dark blue waters.

"This really is a lovely place," she mused aloud. "What's it like here in the winter?"

"Cold, isolated by fog and rough seas some days. Clear, calm and surprisingly warm other times. You have to adapt," he conceded. "But if you're content here, adapting is easy."

She gazed out the window. "I guess that's the key to living anywhere."

Thomas turned off the highway onto a dirt lane leading to a locked gate with a huge No Trespassing sign. He had a key.

"Why do you have a key?" she asked as they got out of the car.

"Because I own this piece of land. Bought it just the other day."

He opened the gate. Katy walked through, and stopped to look around. In the near distance, the tiny arm of the sound glistened fluidly in the sunlight. Dark firs surrounded its curving shore. But what drew her attention were the stones that composed its beach. Small, plump, round, oval stones: white-speckled black and black-speckled white, all worn to satin smoothness by the action of the water.

They were irresistible. Katy began collecting stones with childish glee.

"So many perfect specimens!" She sighed. Hands filled to overflowing, she sank onto a driftwood log. "What a unique place, Thomas! I'm so glad you decided to buy it. If everyone behaved the way I did," she added ruefully, "this would all disappear in no time."

"That's why the sign and locked gate. Can you imagine how long it's taken the sea to round these off?" he asked, sitting beside her. "You may choose three stones."

"Five."

He threw back his head and laughed. "All right, five. But that's it. Hey, do you ski?"

She nodded. "Black slopes."

"Great! I've got a lodge in Tahoe, maybe we could go there sometime. Ski, drink hot chocolate, build roaring fires..."

Her heart twisted and Katy smiled. "That sounds like fun. Karin and I loved to ski. Spending a week or two in Aspen was an annual thing with us, and we—"

"Did you never do anything alone, Katy?"

The abrupt question rattled her. "I—I don't understand what you mean."

"Did you ever do anything by yourself? All I've heard is *we,* not *I*."

"Of course I've done things alone," she told him. "For one, I got married." *And look what a disaster that was,* an inner voice said. Confusion combined with her unease. "Why are you asking me this?" she demanded.

"I think that sometimes," he replied, choosing his words with care, "you bring up Karin as a sort of barrier between us."

She stared at him, then lowered her gaze. "I feel as if I've been blindsided."

"I didn't mean to do that," he responded gently. "I just think it's something you might not be aware of doing."

"That's ridiculous." She blinked, eyes dampening. "I was merely trying to—to share with you how wonderful Karin was."

Thomas retreated to the safety of humor. "Lord, woman, just seeing how wonderful *you* are is enough to dazzle my poor eyes. Any more wonder and I'd be blind!"

She gazed at him consideringly for a moment, then laughed. "I'll try to hold it down, Thomas," came her droll reply. Standing, she dusted off her jeans. "Shall we get on with the tour?"

Eight

Thomas stood by the window looking out on the sodden lawn. The day that had seemed so promising had turned wet and gray by early afternoon. Katy was upstairs with her laptop computer, an almost visible Do Not Disturb sign hanging around her neck. He was lonesome. He felt neglected. And cold. He'd built a fire, but its warmth had not yet become noticeable. He considered turning on a lamp, then promptly forgot about it at the sound of footsteps on the stairs.

Katy swept into the room, accompanied by a wisp of perfume.

"All through?" he asked, helplessly smiling.

"All through. Transcribed, printed out, ready to mail. That photo place you recommended did an excellent job developing my photographs, by the way. The article's still a little rough, but I wanted my editor to read it before I fine-tuned it. She always has good suggestions."

Thomas could only nod. She was wearing designer's overalls and she loosened the straps as she crossed the room. Daintily she stepped out of the denim garment and stood before him clad in a red T-shirt and shimmering red satin bikini panties.

"This has been," she said, winding her arms around his neck, "the most delightful two days of my life. Thank you, Thomas."

He cleared his throat. "You're welcome. You smell so good!" Burying his face in her hair, he held her close and breathed her in until she seemed to fill his entire being.

As if of their own accord, his fingertips began the intimacy of touch, light, erotic strokings to the edge of her shirt. He pulled it up and over her head. Her bra was that same exciting red satin. His fingers continued their play, stopping at tiny barriers of cloth, moving around, under, into.

The deliciously soft tracings on bare, sensitive skin flooded Katy with exquisite pleasure. Aching to give as well as receive, she unbuttoned his shirt and began her own caresses.

His trousers were a hindrance; swiftly he disrobed. Her warm hands found him, making him gasp. Behind them the fire crackled with renewed vigor. Her laugh soft and sultry, she let her head fall back in wanton invitation.

A race of kisses pleasured her throat. "This is wonderful," she murmured.

"Yes, it is," he agreed. "Do you know the real meaning of that word, Katy? It means filled with wonder. And I am. Each time I make love with you, I'm filled with wonder. I need to know—God, I do need to know that you feel that way, too."

Katy felt a flicker of unease at his intensity. But he was drawing her down onto the rug that fronted the fireplace and she lost her worries in the avalanche of sensation. His mouth moved over her, hot, rough velvet on her skin. His hands, strong and sure, molded and shaped her. Their pulses raced and their breaths quickened as heated skin touched heated skin. His hardness fit to her softness, their hearts pounding with excitement, tantalizing them with the promise of ecstasy.

Husky-voiced, he called her name, and she willingly followed wherever he led, deeper and deeper into this sweet fire, until she herself was pure, dancing flame.

"You sleepy?" he asked.

"Very sleepy," she said, proving it with a vast yawn.

They were in bed, floating on a euphoric cloud that had only recently touched earth again. He grinned to himself; such romantic thoughts, Logan! His skin still itched from contact with that blasted rug. And afterward, like some medieval white knight, he had picked her up and carried her to bed, and made love to her again.

Suddenly, he laughed aloud and hugged her. She smelled so good and felt so good! He was compelled to say it. "I love you, Katy."

"No!" Her body tensed. "Please, Thomas, don't. I'm feeling vulnerable enough, as it is. Don't make me regret this." Her voice grew stronger. "I cannot and will not let myself fall in love with you."

"Too late," he replied with insouciant confidence. "I think you already have. In fact, the more I think about it, the more certain I become. In fact, Katy me darlin', I think you're crazy about me."

"And I think you're just plain crazy," she retorted, but he heard the involuntary smile in her voice.

Keep it light, Thomas. Heeding his inner warning, he stretched, yawned. "Shame, Katy," he scolded. "Millions of people search all their lives for love and never find it."

"The only thing I'm searching for is sleep. In vain, I might add."

Her attempt at humor, combined with the tremor in her voice, made him ache. Chuckling, he ruffled her hair. "Okay, okay! Good night, Katy. Sweet dreams."

They settled into their cozily familiar sleeping positions, she on her back, he on his side, his hand light upon her arm. *I love you, Katy.* Thomas repeated the words with a sense of wonder. How strange that what he had struggled not to acknowledge, came so easily now. He ached to hear her speak of love for him. But love, he now knew, was not conditional. True love was a gift, freely given. Given with hope of reciprocation, he conceded, but ideally, the kind of love he wanted was utterly devoid of condition or obligation.

Now, if he could only live up to that ideal, Thomas thought, edging his face into her hair. He was still human, still very much a man with a very healthy ego. And egos, he admitted wryly, demanded to be loved back.

But what he had right now was sublime. Her scent filled his nostrils. Her warmth bridged the space between them and erased any sense of separateness. Lulled by her soft, steady breathing, he drifted into a trance of contentment.

Part of him was aware of her increasingly restless slumber. Now and then her limbs twitched, and soft, inarticulate sounds escaped her lips. When she bolted upright with a groaning cry, Thomas realized he had been expecting it.

He snapped on the lamp. She was hunched over with her face in her hands, struggling to smother the sobs that shook her body.

He reached for her.

She recoiled.

Acting on sheer instinct, he pulled her back to him, a little battle in itself, and held her in a firm embrace.

She slumped against him, defeated by her own tears.

"Shh, Katy, it's all right, love, it's all right," he repeated over and over, knowing full well it wasn't all right. But he felt gallingly helpless to combat her night-terrors.

Her pain tore at him, a physical hurt deep in his chest. He held her and stroked her hair, feeling grossly inadequate.

Regaining control, she said stiffly, "I'm sorry, Thomas."

He sighed. "I'm sorry, too. That nightmare again?"

"It never stops, will never stop!" she said wretchedly.

"Oh, honey, yes it will."

"No. No." She wrenched away from him and stalked to the window, naked, fragile, heartbreakingly vulnerable in the pale moonlight. He went to her.

"Oh, Thomas." She pushed him away, crying, angry. "This is why I can't love you, don't you see? I've lost everyone I've ever cared about, my parents, my grandmother, my sister, everyone! All taken from me, torn from me—God! Don't, Thomas, don't touch me." She huddled into her own arms. "I can't take any more losses." Her voice climbed. "I can't, damn it, I just *can't!*"

Rendered mute by her distress, Thomas touched her shoulders, his palms registering the poignant duality of strength and frailness. He knew what he had to do. He was scared, he admitted. A strong man, he could take on just about anything. Anything except her scorn and disdain. But love made him more determined than ever to breach her defenses.

She shivered. He pulled the sheet off the bed and wrapped it around her. "No one is ever lost to you, Katy," he began.

"Oh, stop with the platitudes," she cut in, her voice ragged with emotion. "I've heard all that stuff before. It didn't help then and it doesn't help now!"

Thomas hesitated, then made his decision. "Katy, I want to tell you something. I've wanted to share this with you for a while, but I wasn't sure how you'd react. But I think it might help now."

Looking confused, she asked, "Tell me what?"

"That there's no reason for you to fear death. This isn't platitudes talking, Katy, it's personal experience. I know this, you see. I know it for a fact."

She eyed him. "What do you mean you *know* it?"

"I mean I died, Katy. I was killed in a car wreck."

His simple statement whitened her face. She sank down on the windowsill, her eyes as wide and grave as a child's. "Thomas, you're frightening me," she whispered.

"I don't mean to." He drew a deep breath. "Are you familiar with the term 'near-death experience'? An NDE?"

"I've read a little about it." She wiped her cheeks. "A very controversial subject, if I remember right."

"Very," he conceded wryly. "I seldom mention it to anyone. But it happened. About four years ago," he forestalled her question. Quickly he skimmed over the accident. "The car plunged through the guardrail, down a deep ravine, and burst into flames before it hit bottom."

"Oh God." She pressed a white-knuckled hand to her mouth.

Hurriedly Thomas went on, "But I was thrown from the car. I recall clearly watching from a vantage point above the scene. Katy, I saw my body fly through the air and land in a patch of brush, broken, battered, but of no more interest to me than a temporary shelter I was leaving behind. I wasn't afraid, I was at peace, honey. Supremely at peace."

He watched her closely, every change of expression, every flicker of eyelash. "Then I emerged into the most fantastic light, Katy! And there were people waiting to welcome me, all radiant, all glowing like that incredible, glorious light!" Urgency frayed his voice as he tried to describe what he'd experienced, for he knew how it sounded even to someone who had "read a little about it." How could he convey his sense of lightness and joy?

She shifted in discomfort, and he read the question she was asking herself. Did he *really* believe this?

"What happened next?" she asked.

Relief swamped him. He didn't see interest and delight on her face, but at least she was listening. "Then I—I was suddenly in a garden, the most beautiful garden, with flowers so brilliant and colorful . . ." He shook his head as he tried to describe it. "So lovely, so exquisitely lovely," he concluded, sighing. "I wanted to stay there forever."

"But you came back."

Their gazes locked. "I came back. I didn't want to, but I was persuaded that I should. Katy, you can't believe the transformational power of that experience," he burst out. "It turned my life upside down, completely changed my values, my priorities— I said you wouldn't have liked me back then and I meant it. I was such a *mercenary*, so obsessed with material things!" He snatched a breath, trying to calm himself, for his words were practically tumbling over each other. "Well? Any comments?" he queried on a quieter note.

Katy drew the sheet up to her chin. "You could have been fantasizing, Thomas," she said gently. "After all, you were in a great deal of pain."

"I don't know," he said, shaking his head. "When I returned to the scene there were ambulances and medical people— I heard myself pronounced *dead*, Katy. But I regained consciousness in the hospital."

"And I'm very glad you did, Thomas." She stood up, wrapped in the sheet like a Grecian goddess. A goddess with a tear-stained face, he thought. He went to her, and this time she let him hold her. "I don't know what else to say," she confessed, her words muffled by his chest.

"You don't have to say anything." He kissed the top of her head. "I had my own purpose for sharing all this with you. I think it's possible that Karin had the same experience, that she felt the same peace I did."

Katy stilled, an alabaster column in his arms. "You mean she . . . she might have been . . ."

"Spared the dreadful pain you envision? Yes, that's exactly what I meant."

"But there's no scientific proof of an NDE," she rebutted softly, yearningly.

"No," he conceded. "But just because it can't be replicated in a laboratory doesn't mean it didn't happen. Personally, I believe it did. It was just so damned *awesome*, Katy! Words can't begin to describe it. Even Carl Jung agreed with that. He wrote that what happens after death is so unspeakably glorious, that our imaginations and feelings do not suffice to form even an *approximate* conception of it!"

"But I still miss her so," she cried after a moment of reflection.

"I know," he murmured. "That's really what grief is, our own personal sense of loss of someone who's left such an aching hole in our life." He lifted her up and carried her to the bed, then settled in beside her. "So, has any of this helped you? Or do you think I'm nuts?" he asked, and held his breath for her answer.

Katy bit her lip. She didn't know what to think. But she had no doubt as to the truth of his conviction.

"I don't think you're nuts. And while I'm not wholly convinced your experience was real and not an illusion," she said carefully, "I don't doubt its validity in your mind. You believe it was real and that's what matters." Her cool, slender fingers caressed his cheek. "I know it must have been tough sharing your story, and I thank you. It has given me a lot to think about."

Thomas just smiled. He had so much more he wanted to say, but she was looking up at him through her lashes, lips parted invitingly. With sudden, searing desire he caught her face and kissed her.

Katy responded with the same surging hunger. They made love sweetly, passionately, with infinite tenderness and wild, swift abandon. Afterward, he held her until he fell asleep.

"What's with the hat?" Thomas asked when she joined him for breakfast the next morning.

"Bad hair day."

"Nothing I've done, I hope?" His grin devilish, he poured her some coffee.

"You certainly didn't help any," she muttered. Flexing her fingers, she heaved a sigh. "I'm a wreck, a total wreck. Just look at these nails. I need a manicure, a pedicure, a haircut."

"This may astonish you, but we have such marvels available right here on the island," Thomas replied cheerily. "Manicurists, pedicurists, hairstylists, at your service."

She stared at him. "You think a woman can go to just *any* hairstylist?" Ignoring his response, she took the steaming mug in both hands and inhaled deeply. "Ah, life in a cup," she said. "You do make good coffee."

"And good love?"

"Adequate. Ouch, Thomas, this coffee is hot!"

Thomas's laughter came from a place deep inside his heart. He was so *happy*. Because he knew she loved him, he acknowledged the source of his joy. Oh, she wouldn't admit it. She was afraid to love him, afraid of the hurt that she believed it would almost certainly cause.

Well, maybe he'd get hurt, too. It was a trade-off, he supposed, one he accepted without a second thought. But would she?

She got up to refill her cup. Eyeing her appreciatively in her red turtleneck and black jeans, he cast about for an entry into the subject uppermost in his mind.

But she had her own agenda for the day. She wanted to go to the post office, and then see some of the mainland. She was quicksilver bright and eager to get going.

Reluctantly, Thomas gave up the idea of spending time alone with her. Although he wanted to discuss their relationship, he decided to wait for her to bring up the subject.

She didn't. By sheer dint of will, he repressed the urge to corner her. "Cool it, Logan," he warned himself. It would take time for a woman like Katy to open herself up to love and he had to give her that time.

"What on earth are you thinking about?" she asked, eyeing his silent, moving lips.

"You," he said glumly, and kissed her. This privilege she had given him, this lovely right to kiss her anytime he wanted, was a rousing delight. He took full advantage of it.

"Thomas...Thomas, we're all dressed and ready to go," she said breathlessly. "There isn't time—"

"There's always time." He claimed her lips again, kissing her until his own breath came in ragged gusts. Her body arched against his, seeking planes and angles to fill its soft hollows. The passion they created together was incredible, he thought in the brief moment before all rational thought ceased. Triumphant, he swept her up in his arms and carried her back to their rumpled bed.

Although they missed the ferry and had to wait for the next one, Katy did get to see the sights. They left the charming port of Anacortes for Desolation Pass, an area famed for its stunning views. She used up several rolls of film, often turning the camera on Thomas, who was himself a marvelous view, Katy thought.

After a quick lunch, they took the ferry again, hopping from island to island.

It was late afternoon when they returned to the house. The minute they stepped inside, Thomas captured her attention with an enticing proposal.

"You look tired. It's a lovely evening, so how about having a light supper outside, just crackers, cheese and wine."

She looked pleased.

"In the hot tub," he added. "Food, flirtation and stimulating conversation. How's that sound?"

"Sounds delicious. You grab some towels and wineglasses, I'll bring the rest. Go on," she said imperiously when he protested. "You've earned a little pampering for being such a good sport today."

Thomas was chin-deep in the churning water when she joined him. He lay with his head against the rim of the tub, eyes half-closed. She had put on her robe. Enthralled, he watched through his lashes as she set down the tray and stripped off the pink garment, to stand before him in another of those scandalous bikini-and-bra sets, shimmering satin, black as night.

When she was settled opposite him, he poured wine and pressed a glass into her hand.

"Thank you. Um, this is nice." She sighed luxuriously, then turned her attention to him. "About this NDE thing, Thomas," she said, reading him like a book. "Surely you found it a *little* disturbing."

"At first, sure. Mainly because of the reaction I got from the few people I told about it. At best they declared it a bad dream, at worst, a mental abberation that might even require psychiatric help," he said ironically.

She touched his thigh with her toes. "Oh, Thomas, can you blame them?" she chided. "You were just coming out of a terrible accident, raving about what even you must admit was a very strange tale."

"It was also the most profound experience I've ever had," he said, then grimaced at his flat tone. "For a time I nearly lost track of that trying to square what I thought with what others thought. Integrating something like this into your regular life is no small task, Katy. When I came here I was one mixed-up man. After I decided to trust myself, I did some investigating, mostly through books. Then I heard about IANDS, which is the International Association for Near-Death Studies. They sponsor support groups across the country, and when I joined one..."

Thomas paused, noting that his body was tense despite the liquid heat. Confiding something so deeply personal made him feel excruciatingly vulnerable. He forced himself to relax. "What I learned is that I'm merely one of many, many people, including little children, who've had this experience."

Her eyes widened. "Little children? Really?"

"Really. But what's so strange about that? Children are resuscitated, too. There are several books that deal just with this subject."

She nodded reflectively, and took a lingering sip of wine.

Sensing her disinterest in pursuing the subject, Thomas smiled as her toes wandered higher up his thigh, then laughed outright when she tickled him intimately. He indulged her sensuous play for a few moments, delighting in it, but impatient, too. He had something else to say before giving himself up to pleasure.

He captured her tantalizing toes. "I hate to break the mood, but we need—*I* need—to get serious for another minute."

Wariness replaced her smile.

"Katy, I know you loved your sister very much. But excessive grief, the inability to let go and get on with your life, can be a heavy burden on someone who also loves you very much." His voice became urgent. "Stop holding on to her, Katy. Let her go, give her peace."

She stared at him, her eyes darkening. With excessive care, she set her glass on the rim of the tub. "That's so cruel, Thomas, so cruel." Her voice shook. "To say that to me, to accuse me of excessive grief, of holding on—

God! And you say you love me?'' She shot to her feet. "Do me a favor and stop loving me, okay?''

"I couldn't stop loving you if I wanted to. And I wasn't being deliberately cruel, you know that,'' he said gruffly. Distressed at her obvious pain, he held out his arms. "Come here, love, let me hold you while I try to explain.''

"I don't want explanations!'' she cried. Wheeling around, she started to get out of the tub. Thomas caught her around the waist and brought her to him in a mighty splash that soaked them both. She spluttered, and shoved her hands against his shoulders. He simply held on to his slippery catch.

Eventually she gave up and went limp. He suspected that some of the water on her lovely face were tears. Regret was dagger-sharp. He pulled her onto his lap and kissed her fiercely.

"Katy, I know you're still grief-stricken over Karin's death—grief is natural. But within limits, honey. Once it crosses certain boundaries, it becomes harmful, both to you, and to your sister's memory.''

Katy put her hands over her face. "I don't know how to respond, I don't know what you want from me, Thomas!'' she cried.

"I want you to open your eyes and *see*. Karin's gone, Katy. You're not. You're here, you're alive and uniquely you. Not half a person, not the other part of Karin. You are *you*. Strong, intelligent, alive in every sense of the word. And life is precious, Katy. You'll be cheating yourself if you don't live every minute of that life to the fullest.''

She sighed, a long, hard exhalation. "Thomas the oracle,'' she murmured wryly.

He pressed his lips to her wet hair. "Thomas the man, who's trying his damnedest to make sense of all this,'' he retorted. "I do think, though, that you need a sense of closure. So come on, talk to me."

"About what?"

"About you and Karin," he said firmly. "Tell me all about you two, starting at birth."

Nine

The winds of Orcas Island had the tang of apple cider, Katy decided, savoring the capricious weather. The first drops of rain splattered against her face and a lovely coolness brushed her bare arms. When the downpour came, she took refuge in the gazebo.

Camera in hand, she curled up on the wraparound bench. She felt so attuned to the elements, so at one with nature. Open and accessible. "Instead of closed up like a clam," she said, poking fun at herself.

When Thomas asked her if she felt any different after their talk, she had replied with rueful honesty, "I don't know, Thomas. I truly don't know."

Although a stubborn inner defiance had caused her to hedge, she had been sincere. A very insistent part of her wanted to believe in the realness of his experience, but she knew that was based more on the circumstances of Karin's death than personal conviction.

Still, she knew a change had taken place within her. The desolating grief she felt for Karin had been gentled somehow. It felt natural, like the chill that comes with a rainstorm even on a summer day. Whatever the cause, she was grateful for the respite.

The rain stopped. Katy closed her eyes, reveling in her solitude. She needed it. Things had gotten pretty intense with Thomas these past few days, Katy acknowledged with a delicious little shiver.

As usual, she was of two minds about this.

One part of her exulted in their intimacy.

The other part set off alarm bells every time she acknowledged its presence.

Thomas. Involuntarily, her lips formed a smile around his name. He was certain she loved him. She had no choice, he'd declared.

It still made her uneasy to hear him speak of love. So she laughed and called him a hopeless romantic. But in truth, she was experiencing some pretty dazzling emotions herself: joy, excitement, passion, and sweetest of all, a rare sense of contentment. All as fragile as a soap bubble, she reminded herself, trying to balance the dangerous happiness swelling her heart as she saw him coming toward her.

He paused. "Am I intruding?"

"No, come in," she invited. His sensitivity pleased her. When she'd said she needed her space, he seemed to understand. At least he hadn't acted wounded by her need for solitude.

"Finish your paperwork?" she asked as he sank onto the bench beside her.

"Most of it." He stretched, and let an arm curve around her shoulders. "You get anything done?"

"I took more pictures. Despite the rain, the light was fabulous, sort of a silver-gold radiance. I want to include this section of the island in my book," she chattered on. "If I ever have a book, that is."

"This is something new," he observed. "What kind of book are you planning?"

"One of those gorgeous, full-color, coffee-table books, the kind you keep forever. Filled with seductive pictures of America at her best. And some beautiful people, too. Smile," she said, turning her camera on him.

His mouth twitched. "Wasting film, Katy," he scolded.

"It's not wasted." Rising, she circled him, snapping pictures while he laughed and protested some more.

He reached up and circled her waist with both hands, bringing her down on his lap. "Behave," he ordered, and kissed her breathless.

Just then, the sun came out, strong, golden shafts of lights raying through the clouds. "Ready to explore?" Thomas asked. "I thought we'd tramp through my woods. You'll love it—giant firs, ferns that come up to your waist. Lots of wildlife, too."

"Small wildlife, I hope," Katy said.

He laughed and affectionately ruffled her hair. Their magic days and nights together had passed like a dream for Thomas. Never had he wanted a woman as much, or as deeply, as he wanted Katy. And she wanted him, he was certain of that.

But he wanted her forever. How did she want him?

He didn't know, and maybe that made him a fool, he conceded. Charging ahead without knowing how she felt wasn't the smartest thing he'd ever done.

Well, it wasn't the dumbest, either, he decided, his spirits soaring again as she slipped her hand into his. True, she still hadn't mentioned love, not even in their most passionate moments. But he was aware of an unfolding taking place. She was blossoming like a flower, and he knew it was only a matter of time before she admitted the truth to herself—and then to him.

At the end of their active day, Katy was more than willing to relax in the kitchen with a light supper of salad and a crusty baguette. Later, they enjoyed the hot tub again, an amorous interlude that culminated in his bedroom.

She had never dreamed that passion could bond two people this way, Katy reflected drowsily. So beautiful and splendid. And so dangerously addictive.

This time their lovemaking had been beguilingly playful. They'd had *fun*. In her experience, sex had always been such a serious business. Who could have guessed that they could laugh and tussle and tease right up to the moment of ecstasy?

Her skin still tingled from his caresses.

Her lips felt wonderfully soft and full, almost swollen, she thought, touching fingertips to her mouth.

She could still taste him, smell him, even see him in her mind's eye. *All marvelous sensations, but purely physical,* she reassured herself. There was no danger in physical pleasure, no chance of being devastated by hurt or grief. She was safe here.

She laid a hand on his chest, her touch light as a feather on his strong physique. He was asleep.

Blissfully fulfilled, she nestled closer and released herself to slumber...

The nightmare began near dawn. This time, Katy didn't cry out or make any kind of noise. She was trapped in a terrible trance, too frozen with horror to move a muscle.

She had to stop the dream, stop it *now,* before it was too late! Fighting her way to the surface of sleep was like wading through deep, sucking mud, every step a life-and-death struggle. Something was following her and she had to outrun it. To confront it would mean the end of everything.

Then it caught her, overtook her. And she could do nothing to stop it from happening again. Nothing!

Katy shot up in bed, stifling her scream before it could escape her trembling mouth. Her entire body shook, she realized. Swift, shallow breaths cadenced her heartbeats and she bit down on her knuckles to keep back the sounds tearing at her throat.

Fearful of waking Thomas, she crept from the bedroom and went upstairs to her own.

She turned on the lamp and sank onto the bed. She was still shaking, still stunned by the depth of her dream.

Cold, clammy, shivering so hard her body ached, she hugged herself, a familiar position that offered no comfort tonight.

Desolation gripped her like steel talons as the nightmare replayed itself. It had been the same agonizing scene: the crashing plane, her desperate attempts to reach it before that red blossom of fire destroyed her world, the horrible, burgeoning awareness that she would fail, again.

Only one thing had changed in her dream. This time, the pilot was Thomas.

"Katy?" Thomas gently shook her shoulder. "Katy, you okay?"

"Thomas, what...oh!" Her startled movement evoked a groan as Katy came awake. Apparently she had cried herself to sleep, in such a rigid position that her bones creaked as she uncurled and turned onto her back. "Yes, of course I'm okay."

"You had another nightmare." He sat down beside her and brushed back her tangled hair.

"Yeah, I did," she admitted with a long sigh. His hand felt so good stroking her cheek.

"Same one?"

Katy's hesitation was imperceptible as she made a lightning-quick decision. "Bad as ever," she replied. "Mmm, you look good." She smiled at him, liking what she saw. He was bare-chested, his dark hair rumpled, strong chin bristly, a cowlick sticking straight up at the back of his head. When he grinned, she was compelled to open the comforter and invite him into her bed, an offer he readily accepted.

Oh, Katy, what are you going to do? She answered her mental question by burrowing into his arms and closing her eyes to reality's harsh light.

It was a poignantly brief respite.

"Go back to sleep," he murmured. "It's only five-thirty. I shouldn't have disturbed you, but I was worried. Waking up to find you gone from my bed is not the best way to start the morning."

Her yawn was meant to suggest compliance. Instead, she was seizing the moment to sort herself out. By omission, she had lied to Thomas. She had wanted to confide in him, but superstitiously wondered if she should. Maybe that would bring him bad luck—maybe her dream was an omen!

Or maybe it was simply the residue of fear forced to the surface, Katy conceded wearily. Whatever it was, the risk was too great. She could not tell him that this time it was not her sister, but he himself who perished in that flaming pyre on the runway.

And she could do nothing to stop it.

A tremendous shudder clawed its way through her body. By sheer willpower, she lay perfectly still, feigning drowsiness. But her heart had stopped, and then lurched into a painful new rhythm as she realized she *could* do something.

She could end this.

The thought was acid on tender flesh. She recoiled from the pain at first, then, her mouth set in bleak resolve, she accepted it. What choice did she have? The possibility of losing Thomas that way was unbearable. It would destroy her.

Besides, what good would you be to him? she asked herself. *He needs a strong woman to share his life, not a fearful creature who can't even share his greatest joy. You'd be doing him a favor.*

Katy shut her eyes to block a new flow of tears. Why the hell did love have to hurt so much?

Her breath snagged as she realized what she had just admitted. She loved Thomas Logan. Too much, too soon, but loved him, all the same. How on earth was she going to walk away from it?

The next two days were exquisite torment for Katy. Determined not to hurt him any more than necessary, she was sweet and affectionate. But the barrier was back between them in the form of a subtle aloofness.

Thomas knew it. He was not fooled by her bright laughter and her delightful willingness to abandon herself to his lovemaking. She was withdrawing the most important part of herself, shutting him out in many little ways.

Frustration and anger began building inside him, a slow burn that was fast becoming a blaze. He tried to tamp it down, but old habits did indeed die hard, he thought sardonically. Accustomed to swift, decisive action that readily resolved problems, he found it extremely difficult to restrain himself.

He tried to discover the reason for her emotional retreat, saying, with a husky laugh, "This is a little scary, isn't it! What we're feeling for each other, I mean—it makes you want to back off and say, 'Hey, am I sure I know what I'm doing?' even though you are one hundred percent sure."

She laughed. "I'd settle for fifty percent sure."

His smile died. "I fail to see the humor in that. In fact, I find it very disturbing. I know exactly how I feel about you. What confuses you, what makes you so uncertain about me? I know you care, Katy. Damn it, I *know* you do. So what is it? What's happened?"

"Of course I care, how could I not? You're a great guy, Thomas. But I...I'm just feeling very confused right now. I have so much on my mind, you've given me so many things to think about."

"Like what?" he asked, watching her carefully.

"Oh, you know what." Becoming aware of her shaky legs, Katy placed a hand on the dining room table for support. "I don't want to discuss this anymore, okay?"

His frustration erupted. "No, it's not *okay!* Dammit, Katy, talk to me, tell me what's wrong. One minute we're close and intimate and happy, the next you're encased in ice. I've tried breaking through it, I've tried so hard it hurts. But you keep shutting me out, holding me at arm's length. After the way I opened up to you, literally bared my soul—do you have any idea how much trust that entailed? But I wanted so much to help you overcome your fears..." He ran a hand roughly over his face. "At least tell me why you keep pushing me away!"

Katy's heart contracted painfully. "Thomas, I'm sorry, I don't mean to hurt you—"

"Then stop doing it. Stop running away!"

"I'm not running, I'm..." Despair and anger fought for precedence. Anger won. Her chin snapped up. "I told you how I felt about love, I told you over and over! But you don't listen, you never listen to anything you don't want to hear!"

Shaking like a leaf inside, she unflinchingly met his hot-blue gaze. "You're too accustomed to being the boss, taking charge, having things go exactly the way *you* think they should. Well, you don't always get everything your way, Thomas. You're not the CEO here. My opinions, my feelings, are just as valid as yours!"

He drew back as if she had slapped him. "Did I ever, for one minute, imply that they weren't?" he asked bitterly. When she did not reply, he added, "Maybe you're right about me not listening, though."

"Maybe it's time you started, Thomas."

His fingers clenched as if physically grappling with his emotions. "Maybe it is," he said, eyes hard and glinting. "Maybe it's also time I stopped doing so much *feeling* and started doing more *thinking*." Wheeling, he strode across the room and out the back door.

Katy held fast to the table's smooth surface to stop herself from running after him. Only when she heard his truck start up did she bring her hands to her wet face.

"Oh, darling, I'm sorry," she whispered as she heard the squeal of his tires peeling out of the driveway.

The things she had wanted to say to him were tumbling around her throat like sharp-edged stones. Calling Patsy was almost a reflex; they had poured out their young hearts to each other many a time.

"Patsy, I really need to talk. True confession time," she said with a rather pathetic attempt at humor. "Are you game?"

"Oh, Katy, of course I am," came Patsy's soft assurance.

Her green eyes bright with curiosity, Patsy was waiting on the minuscule porch when Katy drove up.

"Just like old times," she murmured as they walked into each other's arms. Her voice was uneven; she cleared her throat. "Come inside, sweetie-pie heart. Sit down, I made ginger tea."

The old, familiar endearment made Katy chuckle in spite of her heartache. Sitting across from her friend in the kitchen alcove, she sipped the pungent tea until she could begin.

"I love Thomas," she said.

"Oh!" Patsy started up, then sank back down. "Oh. Hold the applause, huh?" She sighed. "What happened?"

"What happened is that I didn't want to fall in love and then I did and I was happy for a little while..." Katy gulped air. "Then I had that nightmare again, only this time it was Thomas dying in that plane crash and I couldn't take it, Patsy, I just could not take it!"

Patsy wisely kept silent.

"So then I tried to pull back, stop what I'd foolishly allowed to get started. I did it nicely, I pretended all was well while I cast about for a way to break it off without hurting him."

"But he saw right through that."

"He saw through it. We had a fight and he stormed out of the house." Katy swiped at her tears. "End of story."

"Oh, nonsense, of course it isn't the end. You just tell him what you told me. He'll understand, honey."

"I can't tell him. Oh, damn it all anyway!" Katy cried. "How can I tell him I saw his plane crash? How can I even put that idea in his mind?"

Patsy eyed her, plainly puzzled. "I'm missing something. Why can't you tell him? Oh! You mean you're afraid he'll crash just because you... I didn't realize you were so superstitious, Katy."

"Usually I'm not, but about this, yes, blast it, I am. Patsy, you told me you believe that dreams are messages. Well, what if it's true, what if this dream is a message? An omen, even! You've heard of self-fulfilling prophecies! And there's my record for losing loved ones to consider. I could bring him bad luck just by being around him, for God's sake!"

"Surely you don't believe that!"

"It's possible. It's even possible that I... Patsy, I've begun to think that I'm cursed."

"So why are you around me, then?" Patsy asked reasonably. "Or don't you love me?"

"Oh, of course I love you." Katy dropped her face into her hands. "Maybe I am being foolish, I don't know," she said wearily. "But what if I'm not? After all the strange things Thomas has told me, who's to say what's nonsense and what's reality? Or could become reality, if I let it. How can I knowingly take that risk? I can't, you know that. Even worse, I know it, too. The only thing is . . ." Bleak violet eyes stared into the distance. "Patsy, where am I going to get the strength to do this?"

Katy returned to the inn around nine that evening. Thomas wasn't home. Since it was still light, she rambled around his vast grounds, hoping to finally expend her energy.

Lost in thought, she tramped through fields and forest, miraculously ending up at her starting point in the garden. It was after ten and the light was fabulous, not daylight, not darkness, but something enchantingly in between. She felt the ache of its loveliness deep in her soul.

For hours she lay awake in bed, her body soft and weak with longing. Thoughts of Thomas whirled in her mind like snow on some fake winter scene in a belljar.

"How can I give him up?" she whispered, hugging her pillow as all her many desires coalesced into fierce, raw need. She wanted to cry and couldn't. She craved the blessed reprieve of slumber. But it was a long time coming. The first golden glow of dawn lit the room before her eyes closed.

She had just fallen asleep, when a hard, rapid knock on her door roused Katy. She blinked and sat up, bleary-eyed, her wits dulled by unrelieved fatigue.

"Katy? You awake?" Thomas called, rapping on the door again.

The urgency in his voice pierced the haze surrounding her senses. "Coming!" Katy said. Her red-eyed image in the full-length mirror made her wince as she crossed the room. Raking shaky fingers through her hair, she jerked open the door. "Thomas? What's wrong?"

"There's a message for you on my machine, from a Dr. Vance."

"Stewart called here? What on earth for?" she asked, not yet making a connection.

"Katy, it's about Nell. Her heart, honey. I'm so sorry to have to wake you like this," Thomas blurted out, hurting inside as she paled.

"Oh, no, no, not Nell, too!" Katy whispered. She swayed, her face a mask of grief.

Too late, Thomas realized the dire interpretation she had put on his words. He caught her in his arms. "No, honey, no, she's not dead! God, I'm sorry, Katy, she's ill, yes, she's had a heart attack, but she's alive, in Intensive Care, being monitored very carefully, Dr. Vance said. He's already left the hospital, but you can call him at home. I'll go get the answering machine and you can hear his message for yourself."

Lowering her into the rocking chair, Thomas ran downstairs. Katy clasped her shaking hands. Her heart knocked against her rib cage in a painful new rhythm and she still couldn't breathe right. Unable to sit for long, she hurried to the closet and grabbed her suitcase with every intention of leaving for California in the next ten minutes.

Thomas returned, and immediately rewound the tape. The doctor's message did little to calm her. As soon as it ended, Thomas dialed the number Dr. Vance had left; Katy's fingers were shaking too badly.

"Thank you," she mouthed, taking the receiver. "Stewart, hello! What happened? How bad is it, is she going to be all right?"

Her shoulders relaxed as she listened to his response. Nell had indeed suffered a heart attack. "A myocardial infarction that caused some mild damage, but overall her prognosis is good," Katy repeated the doctor's reassuring words to Thomas as she handed him the receiver.

"Katy, I'm so glad," Thomas said huskily. He replaced the receiver and sat on the edge of her bed.

"You and me both!" She blew out a breath. "Her condition has stabilized but she's still under observation. Stewart doesn't think she's in any danger, thank God. But I must go to her—oh, Thomas, Nell has no family, either. She's all alone in that hospital room. No one's there for her when she needs it most!"

"Sounds to me like *Stewart* is there for her. Apparently, he's more than just your doctor," Thomas observed.

"Yes, we're friends," Katy said distractedly. "I've got to pack, get dressed, get out of here. What time is it? And what time is the next ferry?"

"It's eight thirty-five."

He paused to clear his throat. Katy was already gathering garments from her dresser drawers and her short white knit nightgown rode up to breathtaking heights when she bent over.

"Katy, I realize you want to get home to Nell as quickly as possible, so I suggest—"

"I'll drive, Thomas," she interrupted, knowing before he said it what he was going to say. "I guess that sounds silly to you, given the situation, but I've got all I can handle right now without challenging myself with a plane ride."

"Nothing you do sounds silly to me," came his quiet rebuttal. "It is a long way, though. Days by car instead of mere hours by plane. And you're upset, to boot."

"I'll be fine. Nell's not in any immediate danger and she knows I'll be home quick as I can." Evading his exasperated look, she said with sharp finality, "Thank you for the offer, but I'll drive."

Thomas sighed and raked a hand through his hair while he considered her refusal. The tempest-like anger that drove him from her side yesterday had blown itself out overnight. His loss of temper still bothered him and even worse, he wasn't sure that it wouldn't happen again. Over the years, he had become very good at controlling his emotions; rarely did anyone ruffle Thomas Logan's feathers.

But rarely was he hit by such raging torrents of emotion. He was overwhelmed by her feminine charm, overwhelmed by his need for her and positively buried under the love that had rolled over him like an Alpine avalanche. He couldn't let her walk out of his life. Hell, without her he didn't even *have* a life. She was the difference between the dreary, gray chill of winter, and summer's bright, golden warmth.

So what do I do now? Surely not lock her in the attic and keep her here forever, he thought sarcastically. The answer came from his own heart. *Respect her wishes. Remember that her feelings and opinions, regardless of what you think of them, are as valid as your own.*

She had made that clear enough, he reminded himself grimly.

With swift, fleet movements she continued packing her suitcase. She was in profile, and the lovely, sculpted lines of her features were heartachingly pure and clean in the sunlight. He clenched his fists to restrain his need to take her in his arms, and hold her, love her, take command of the situation . . .

Damn it, Logan, you have to honor her decisions whether you agree with them or not!

Once again a savage gale of frustration swept through him. It ground him down, forced him to take action—any kind of action.

"I'll make some coffee and toast. You can't start out without breakfast," he said with a ragged touch of his old authority.

She gave him a quick smile.

He turned and strode from the room, his answering machine under his arm. There were other messages, but he had stopped listening after hearing Dr. Vance's voice. *Stewart,* he amended, and gave a harsh laugh. Now he was jealous of a man he'd never even met.

After making fresh coffee, he slipped bread into the toaster. Then he listened to the rest of his messages. A moment later he was taking the stairs two at a time.

"Katy!" he called before he ever reached her open door. "Katy!"

She met him in the hall with her anxious question. "What, Thomas? What's wrong?"

"Nothing about Nell," he said quickly. "I had another message on my machine—the ferry crashed into the dock early this morning and damaged the dock's hydraulics system. Honey, I'm sorry, but right now, the only way you can get off this island is by plane."

Ten

Katy's first reaction was an explosive little laugh of disbelief. "You've got to be kidding! You are, aren't you?" Her voice began to rise as he just stared at her, grim-faced. "Thomas? Oh, please, you're not serious, are you?"

"I wish I wasn't, but, yes, I'm serious. Katy, I called and checked for myself. The official announcement is that the ferry should be running again by noon. But to quote a friend's private opinion, don't bet on it."

"No, I can't believe that! Damn it, it's just too... too—" She flung up her hands in a gesture of frustration. "Just too much of a coincidence!"

"No coincidences, Katy," he reminded her quietly.

Momentarily at a loss for words, she strode back inside her bedroom. A glance at the clock increased her agitation. "It's barely nine o'clock! And I'm supposed to sit around until *noon* waiting for a ferry?"

He shrugged and shoved his hands into his pockets. "That's about it. I'm sorry, Katy."

Her mouth softened. "Oh, Thomas, you have nothing to be sorry for, it's not your fault." She inhaled a breath and forcefully expelled it. The sleeves of her robe fell back to reveal her firm, round arms as she swept both hands through her hair. "I can't just sit here, I'm going to see for myself."

"I'll drive you," he said.

"Thank you, Thomas. I'll get dressed and meet you downstairs."

He nodded. His face was impassive as he walked out the door. But a nagging thought entered his brain. *Not too long ago you wouldn't have had to leave the room while she dressed.*

He wondered if she was just still angry about the fight they'd had last night. He hoped so; a heartfelt apology would bridge that rift. But the distance between them felt more like a chasm, he thought unhappily. Mere words could not span that chasm. He didn't have the words to even try, Thomas acknowledged as he walked out on the patio to wait for her.

A few minutes later, clad in jeans and a pink-checked shirt, she joined him downstairs.

They took his truck. She sat in silence, her hands clasped tightly in her lap. His covert glances at her face made him as anxious as she obviously was. He didn't know what to say to her alabaster profile.

When they reached the landing, the long line of cars waiting for ferry service reinforced his message. They couldn't get near the dock. "Looks like a lot of people are stranded here," he commented.

"Yes, looks like it." *But they can fly out.* Defeated, feeling the onset of a headache, Katy sighed and rubbed her temples. "Let's go back," she said dully.

Without a word, he turned the truck around and drove home.

Her headache in full force, Katy went to her room and
swallowed two aspirin, then resumed packing. It didn't
take nearly long enough. She sat down in the rocker and
tried to resign herself to waiting. Her eyes felt hot and dry.
The tears were there, surging just below the surface, but
she was too stunned and heartsick to cry. She felt so helpless and out of control.

She couldn't sit still. She got up and paced, fumed, even
swore now and then. Nothing helped, nothing soothed her
seething impatience.

At times she heard Thomas moving around downstairs.
The back door slammed as he went outside to empty veg-
etable scraps onto the compost heap. Tears breached the
dam and flooded her eyes as she watched him through the
window. The urge to call him was very strong. Anxiety and
concern gnawed at her until she felt a desperate need for
the comfort of his arms.

Maybe he could even relieve this heavy sense of guilt she
felt, she thought longingly. She shook her head. She didn't
deserve relief. She hadn't been there for her sister. And
now, for the first time, Nell needed *her* instead of the other
way around. "And where am I? Stuck on an island because I can't get on a plane!"

Scourging herself was futile. Besides, hadn't Stewart told
her that Nell was in no imminent danger? Unless, of
course, he hadn't been completely truthful with her. Realizing she would get upset, he might have toned down the
truth . . .

Oh, I'm being silly—Stewart wouldn't lie to me! Irritably she dialed the office number of Nell's doctor, and was
put right through. Stewart merely repeated his prior message; Nell was still in the Intensive Care Unit and was
resting comfortably. He spoke condescendingly, and her
annoyance mushroomed.

"Katy, since you insist on driving instead of flying—"

"My car is on this island, too, Stewart," she said tersely, "and I can't get the damn thing off without a working ferry!"

Unperturbed, he continued, "I'll give you my pager number so you can check in with me at night."

Instantly contrite, Katy thanked him and replaced the receiver. Then, despite Maddie's protests, she cleaned the bathroom until it fairly sparkled.

At noon Thomas prepared lunch.

To her credit, she tried to eat.

To his credit, he kept his mouth shut even though it was killing him to. He had done enough damage already, spewing out his opinions so freely. *And you'd had an opinion on everything,* he reminded himself harshly.

After a few bites of her omelet, Katy put down her fork. "This is a lovely lunch, Thomas. I wish I could do it justice, but I..." She shook her head. "I called the doctor again. He said about the same thing as he said this morning—I'm not to worry. But I keep wondering if he might not be holding something back."

Casually, Thomas asked, "Why would he do that?"

"Well, he knows how I worry... Oh, I'm probably not thinking too clearly. But I just feel so helpless, you know? Like everything's been yanked out of my control again and there's not a damn thing I can do about it," she said. "God, I hate that!"

"A helluva feeling," he agreed.

She eyed him, her mouth tilting ever so slightly. "You have an answer for that, too?"

He had to say it. "As a matter of fact, I do. We can't control what happens in our world, true enough. But we can control how we react to it."

"Unfortunately, what works for you doesn't always work for others."

Despite the lightness of her response, it held a hint of reproof. "It doesn't always work for me, either," he said. "Katy, I'm sorry about last night—"

"Oh, Thomas, please, you don't owe me an apology," came her quick protest.

"Well, I sure as hell owe *some*body one," he said roughly. "Because I know, now, what love is and what it isn't." His darkened gaze leveled to hers. "Love isn't possessive or demanding, and it certainly isn't conditional. You don't owe me a damn thing, Katy. My love is a gift with no strings attached. If I expect more, that's my problem. And whether or not you accept it in no way affects that gift."

Katy didn't know what to say. Mercifully, the silence was brief. "I accept your apology," she said finally. She crumpled her napkin and stood up. Anything else she said would only make things worse. "Well, if you'll excuse me, I think I'll call the hospital."

"I'll check the ferry office."

The quick, boyish smile accompanying his offer sent an arrow of longing through Katy's heart. "Thanks," she replied, holding her embattled self in tight restraint. Carrying a mug of fortifyingly strong, hot coffee, she returned to her room.

Intensive Care did not give out information about patients. Resignedly Katy sat down in the rocker and folded her hands. A moment later she jumped up and grabbed the telephone again. She had forgotten to call Patsy.

Her friend's expressed sympathy and compassion, though deeply appreciated, left Katy feeling worse than ever. Aimlessly she paced the room, then finally took refuge in the comforting old rocker again. Depressed and hurting, she sat wrapped in brooding thoughts for what seemed an incredibly long time.

"Katy?" Thomas rapped on her open door with his knuckles, startling her.

Her heart sank as she noted his somber expression.

"It's not good," he answered the question in her eyes. In a firm, even voice he gave her the latest news. The damage to the dock was greater than anticipated and estimated repairs would take another day, possibly more.

Katy's composure shattered. "Oh, Thomas! The day's nearly gone and I'm still on this blasted island and now you're saying it'll be tomorrow or maybe even ..." She uncoiled from the chair and caught his arm. "Thomas—Thomas, I have to get to Nell, I *have* to—she needs me! I'm all she has, don't you see? Oh, please help me."

Her plea struck Thomas a jarring blow. "Katy, there's only one way I can help you, you know that."

She turned away, then wheeled to face him again. Her violet eyes sparkled with tears. They coated her lashes and splashed down her cheeks as she found a solution. "I know, I'll leave my car here and take a boat to the mainland! I can rent a car in Anacortes, can't I?" She caught his arm again in pleading demand. "Oh, please, Thomas, can you find me a boat?"

With a weary sigh, Thomas captured her hands and brought them to his chest. "A boat, maybe, but a car? Katy, the ferry crash happened hours ago, I doubt there's a rental car left in the entire area. There weren't that many to begin with. I know you're desperate to go to Nell. But at the moment, the only way to do that is by plane."

Her shoulders slumped, and he couldn't stand it.

"Look, if you can trust me enough to at least let me fly you to Seattle, you can rent a car there."

Wincing at what he implied, Katy cried, "I do trust you, Thomas. I *do!*"

A smile touched his mouth in gentle denial of her claim.

She bit her lip, agonized with indecision. Slowly, with visible effort, she drew herself to a tense column of resolve.

"All right, I'll fly to Seattle with you. At least I'll try," Katy said.

"Good for you! I'll help you, it'll be all right." Thomas hugged her, then wrapped his arms around her slim shoulders. "You know, we could skip Seattle altogether and leave from here. My jet just happens to be sitting in the hangar today—synchronicity again," he added, smiling. "We'd arrive within hours instead of days."

Startled, she asked, "You'd go with me?"

"Sure, I could arrange to go with you. It makes a lot more sense than that long drive alone," he said matter-of-factly.

Katy leaned into his embrace. "Why are you so blasted *logical?* Oh God." She sighed, daunted by the thought of spending hours in a small aircraft. "I'm so afraid, Thomas, maybe more than you realize. It's very possible that I'll make a fool of myself, embarrass me, embarrass you..."

"Hey, I'll risk it if you will." Thomas tipped up her chin. "I'll be right beside you, Katy, every second, all the way."

"Do you have any idea how important that is to me? As much as I want to be with Nell, I don't think I could do this with anyone else. Just you, Thomas. You're the only reason I can ever attempt flying," she said with stark candor. "The things you've told me, the way you feel about things I find so frightening..." She shook her head. "Evidently, you've had even more of an effect on me than I realized."

A smile flashed across his face as she spoke. It warmed her. Holding his deep blue gaze, she stated, "You said it took something as profound as a near-death experience to change your outlook on life, but all I needed was you. My courage, what there is of it, comes from you, Thomas."

"You shortchange yourself. From what I've heard, you're one of the bravest women I've ever had the privilege of meeting," he answered, his voice gruff because she had touched him so deeply. "Let me make some calls, file a flight plan, get the jet fueled up, clear my schedule. An hour, no more. Then we'll be on our way."

By the time they reached the airport, Katy's fear was palpable, a small, wild beast trapped in her chest. At the same time, she was eager to get started. An impossible contradiction, she despaired. Using all her resources, she maintained her composure despite the nerves slamming her stomach. But those nerves were vicious. White-faced, swallowing hard to contain her rising nausea, she buckled herself into the seat of the sleek, elegant, appallingly small plane.

"Okay, honey?" Thomas asked.

Katy nodded. She settled back in the seat beside him, rearranged her blazer, returned his easy smile. When he started the engine, she jumped, trembling, her nausea increasing until she thought she would choke on it.

Clenched fists held her terror in check as they roared down the runway. The plane lifted into the air, rising swiftly, circling the airport already so far below.

It was too much for Katy.

Smoothly, Thomas placed an airsickness bag on her lap.

Katy fought desperately against using it, a tiny success that she held on to with all her might. When the plane made a sickening swing to the right, the wraparound windshield gave her the sensation of sitting exposed and naked up in the sky without any means of support. Panic hit her, raw, cold and liquid. Sweat wet her palms. Her breath shortened; dizzied, she grabbed the armrests.

"No, please, please, I can't, Thomas, I can't!" she cried.

Her voice was thin, shrill and breathless. Thomas's swift glance at her face confirmed his fear. Her skin was waxen, and her lips had taken on a faint bluish tint. She was beginning to hyperventilate.

"Katy, control your breathing," he ordered. "Katy? Katy! Listen, listen to me now. Look at the cockpit lights, the instrument lights. Concentrate on the lights. Breathe slowly... slowly, smooth, even breaths. Come *on*, Katy, breathe," he said sharply. "That's better, yes, that's it."

His hand settled tightly over her small fists. "Slow and smooth, in, out, slow and smooth... Now, deep breaths, remember? Just like we talked about on the way to the airport. Deep, deep breaths. Inhale... now hold it... one... two... three... release. Try it again. Inhale, deep, deep... hold. One... two... three... release."

Impossible to ignore, his commanding voice penetrated her paralyzing fear. Katy mentally began repeating his instructions, dragging in deep drafts of air and pushing it out while she clung to his hard, warm hand.

Gradually, her jarring heartbeat eased. Her nausea retreated, bubbling just beneath her rib cage. For a time she simply concentrated on pulling air in and pushing it out.

"Talk to me," she said when she regained use of her voice. "Tell me about your childhood."

Thomas squeezed her icy fingers. "I was a typical boy. I loved fishing, hated girls and baths," he responded lightly. Hope swelled in his chest. Despite her initial reaction, she was doing far better than he expected. His voice was calm and mellow as he continued describing his quite uneventful life as a child.

Vivid and entrancing, details of his experience as yet unheard poured into Katy's ears. She listened in silence. In spite of her rapt attention, every bone in her body ached from the extreme tension that prevented relaxation or even movement. Her mouth was bitter from the acrid taste of fear. But she had managed to retain control of herself, and for that she gave heartfelt thanks.

Lulled by his soothing voice, she closed her eyes and tried to relax her stiff muscles.

An hour or so later, as if to further test her mettle, they ran into a storm. Her breathing became quick and shallow again and she nearly drove her nails through the armrests as the plane began to pitch and yaw.

"Just a minor front, Katy, some dark clouds, a little wind and rain. Nothing to worry about, not in this baby," Thomas said soothingly.

Despite his assurance, Katy had to grit her teeth to keep from crying out as they entered a particularly menacing cloud. She scowled at his unconcerned face. In his opinion, the plane rode this awful turbulence with praiseworthy smoothness, given its size. In *her* opinion, they were bouncing around wildly and could go down at any second.

To her surprise, she didn't panic. But she did groan as the plane dropped with a stomach-turning lurch.

"We'll be out of this in a few minutes, honey," he said. "You okay?"

"Am I okay?" Katy gave a strangled laugh. "I'm sitting here beside you, in the worst possible scenario and I'm thinking, 'Well, at least we'll go together!' So you tell me, am I okay?"

"Of course you are! I told you, you're a strong woman. I've noticed a few other traits I like, too, courage, honesty, good old-fashioned spunk—"

"You're insane. I'm so scared I couldn't stand up if I had to," she said shortly. "And if I had any spunk, I wouldn't be in this situation in the first place. I'd be on a big plane, not this puddle-jumper! And what on earth makes you think I'm courageous?"

"Oh, Katy," he said gently. "Why are you so hard on yourself? Would you come down this hard on anyone else? Your sister? Patsy? Or Nell?"

"Well, no, of course not. Damn! Sometimes you get me so confused, Thomas." She sighed. "The reason I'm so hard on myself is that I'm trying to apply that wise old axiom, *Know thyself*."

"Then you're failing," he said bluntly. "Katy, you haven't the faintest idea what a marvelous piece of work you are. My God, you've had trauma piled on top of trauma, yet you're still here, still persisting, still trying to make a life for yourself."

Katy's reply was arrested by another stomach-turning drop as the plane plunged through a sheet of rain. "I had no other choice," she said tersely.

Thomas argued the point while she shut her eyes and prayed.

The turbulence lessened. Suddenly, incredibly, the flight became silky-smooth. Opening her eyes, Katy gasped with delight as they emerged from clouds into a celestial blue sky.

"Oh, God," she whispered.

"You all right, darlin'?" Thomas asked.

"Yes, I— Yes, I am all right," Katy replied with a startled note of awareness. His quick, warm touch drew her gaze to his face. Looking at him, so big and solid, his strong hands competent and sure on the controls made her feel safe. "I'm all right because I'm with you. Oh, Thomas, you've been so good for me!"

"The feeling's mutual, Katy." His jaw tightened. "So, why have you withdrawn from me? We were so wonderfully close, I've never been that close to anyone before. To me, it was sheer magic. But what was it to you?"

"Magic," Katy said simply.

"Then why did you reject it?"

"I had a good reason," she defended.

His sharp glance stung like a wasp.

"Oh, all right, I'll tell you. The other morning, when you found me sleeping in my own bed, I told you I'd had another nightmare. That was true. What I didn't tell you was who I dreamed about. It was you, Thomas. In my dream it was *your* plane that crashed and burned on that runway. It was horrible!'' She shuddered. ''Just horrible.''

''And you couldn't tell me that? Why the hell not, Katy?''

Jolted by his tone, she replied, ''Because I... I was afraid it would bring you bad luck.''

''Bad luck? You think *you* could cause me to have an accident? Oh, Katy!'' Relief, in the form of laughter, laced his voice. His hand covered both of hers like a warm hug. ''Sorry to deflate your ego, Katy, my love, but you're not that powerful.'' He laughed again and kissed her palm.

''Oh, Thomas,'' she said after a long, considering silence. ''All I know is that when you lose someone, it hurts to be the one left behind.''

''So what's your solution? Crawl in a hole and hide from life? Will that keep you safe from hurt?''

She wrinkled her nose at him. ''You tell me, you're the one with all the answers.''

''All right. I think you have to risk it. It's scary, sure. But the answer to fear is something much more powerful. Love. To love with all your being. It might not stop your fear, but it *will* give you the strength to overcome it.''

''Good answer, preacher.'' Her grin faded. ''In theory, anyway. But in reality... I can't bear the thought of losing you, Thomas,'' she said very softly. ''You mean so much to me that I—I just couldn't stand to go through all that again.''

Eleven

Thomas's heart did a heady somersault. But his ready response died on his lips as he applied her words to his own emotions. How could *he* bear to lose *her*? How could he cope with such a devastating void in his life?

And it would be devastating, he thought. Good Lord, no wonder his feelings for her scared the devil out of him! He'd had no experience with this level of emotion between a man and a woman, no way to prepare himself for being in love.

Another realization swept through him like a keening wind. He had no personal experience with loss, either, but he'd been awfully damn quick to dish out advice to someone who'd had enough grief for several people.

He said slowly, huskily, "In all honesty, I don't know how I could live without you in my life, Katy. I'm trying so hard to practice what I preach, so to speak. But I do know I love you. And to me, that's worth taking any risk, paying any price, for the privilege of spending the rest of my life with you. However long or short that will be doesn't matter. Up here, down there, wherever I am, I want you beside me."

"Oh, Thomas." Katy heaved a heartfelt sigh as joy, honey-sweet and extremely persuasive, filled her to overflowing. With him, all things seemed possible.

"I love you, too, darling." Her mouth quirked. "As you well know. I guess I was never very good at hiding that. And God, yes, I want to be with you! But I haven't changed all that much, I'm still a mess, still riddled with fears. The deepest one, of course, is the fear of loving and losing. It might not be sensible, but it doesn't have to be. It just *is*. My phobia about flying is all mixed up with that. Only the fact that someone I love is sick and scared and terribly alone got me into this plane. And the fact that it's your plane, of course. I need time, Thomas, time to unravel and then resolve this confusion. Otherwise, how can I make a lasting commitment?"

She tilted her head. "That *is* what you're asking for, isn't it? A lasting commitment?"

"A forever kind of commitment," Thomas confirmed, expelling a long breath. "Katy, as you might have figured out by now, I'm not the most patient man when things don't go my way. I never was. I guess what I'm trying to say is, I love you, and I'll give you all the time you require."

He meant it, Thomas assured himself. He'd give her whatever she needed, no matter the cost to himself. He hoped with all his heart he could keep that promise. To himself he gave a brisk little shake. "So okay. Do you want me to hang around San Diego for a while? I could even fly back for you. When you're ready to return, of course."

"Oh, Thomas!" She laughed and touched his cheek, her fingertips soft and cool on his skin. "No, I don't want you to hang around, I've got to give Nell all my attention right now. You don't have to return for me, either. Getting back to Orcas is my problem, not yours."

"But I want to *make* it my problem," he said vehemently.

"And I'd love to hand it over to you," she told him. "But that wouldn't resolve anything. You know, there'll be times when I have to go it alone, Thomas." She sighed, her gaze wistful as she confessed, "And I'm not sure I can. In fact, I'm not sure of anything. Except that I love you."

"And that's not enough?"

"That, my love, is what I have to find out for myself," Katy said with a catch of her heart.

"Must you go out in this weather?" Katy asked, frowning as Nell gathered up her purse and tote bag.

The soft, dark eyes Katy loved so much flashed their exasperated message. *Stop coddling me, Katy!*

Katy flushed. "Well, Nell, it's only been a month since you came home from the hospital. At least take your raincoat and umbrella, it's going to rain."

"It might, but I doubt I'd melt. Katy, dear, please think about what we talked about at breakfast," Nell requested, her tone tart-sweet. She kissed Katy's cheek. She took the umbrella, smoothed her salt-and-pepper cap of fluffy curls and walked out the door, her small frame fairly bristling with purpose.

Eyes soft with love, Katy shook her head as the older woman eschewed the elevator and took the stairs down to the lobby. Nell had become a fitness enthusiast and in a short time her figure had gone from short and stout to short and pleasingly plump. If possible, she walked instead of drove, took a senior citizens' aerobics class three times a week and was considering working out with weights for twenty minutes twice a week. All with doctor's approval, Katy reminded herself whenever she became anxious about Nell's new health routine.

After pouring herself another cup of coffee, Katy strolled through the quiet rooms in restless search of something that had no name. With its waterfront view, the three-bedroom condominium was choice property. It was bright and airy, with touches of luxury in its coffered ceilings and tiled floors, French doors and even a handsome brick fireplace.

Katy already had a serious buyer. But she was loath to sign the papers. Slowly, reflectively, she walked past the pair of lounge chairs where she and Karin had eaten popcorn and watched every movie Audrey Hepburn had ever made, past the windowed nook where the Christmas tree always stood, down the hall with its many framed photographs.

So many precious memories, she thought as she opened the door to her sister's bedroom. Decorated in harmonizing shades of lavender and blue, it looked as though Karin had just stepped out and would return at any minute. Her alarm clock ticked on. Her closet and shelves were still crammed with clothing. Up until now, Katy had been unable to bring herself to clear out the room.

Karin's tattered old teddy bear sat in the pale blue wing chair by the window. Katy caressed its furry head as she gazed around the shadowed room. Even six weeks ago she would not have been up to this painful task. But it's time, she told herself. Empty boxes sat stacked and ready to be filled with her sister's belongings. With firm resolve that cracked only now and then, she began the task.

She worked methodically, folding and placing garment after familiar garment in boxes to be given to charity. When the closet was empty, she began on the dresser drawers.

Her mind wandered along its favorite path. What was Thomas doing right now, right this second? She hadn't seen him since kissing him goodbye at the airport. Five long weeks. *God, how I miss him!*

She'd called him once, to tell him Nell was out of the hospital and doing well. Their conversation had been stiff and awkward. Strangled by too many unsaid words on her part, she acknowledged.

Thomas, his patience strained but still intact, was waiting for her to make a decision. But how long would he wait? He'd said he would give her all the time she needed, and she trusted that. But still, everyone had limits.

There were a lot of good reasons that she had made no plans to return to Orcas, Katy thought. But her ready explanation fell short this time. "Okay, Katy, what's keeping you here?" she asked aloud. "What's the main problem? Besides Nell, that is?"

Of course, Nell was a very *big* problem. It had never entered Katy's mind that the housekeeper might not want to leave San Diego. But Nell, it seemed, was a busy woman. *I've got a life here, Katy. Now why don't you go get yourself one?* she'd said this morning.

Remembering, Katy muttered, "How can I go off again and leave her? What if she has another heart attack? In the middle of the night, no one around to help. Or what if she falls and maybe breaks a hip? She's all alone, who's going to help her?"

Katy had to smile at the melodramatic scenario she was concocting. But she was worried. She would never forgive herself if something happened to Nell...

She smiled, imagining Thomas's response to that. *More guilt, Katy? Why stop there, why not take on responsibility for the whole world?*

Her smile became soft with affection. Reflecting on some of the things he had said helped ease her heartache, whether or not she agreed with him.

But maybe he was right. Certainly he had been on target about her dependent relationship with her sister. She had unconsciously considered herself half a person without Karin.

Even *with* Karin, as Thomas had so adeptly pointed out, she had never considered herself whole.

Her relationship with her husband hadn't been much different, Katy admitted. She had walked in what she'd thought was the shadow of his brilliance. Never his equal. Never her own person. But that was changing. Lately she had felt more balanced, more in harmony with her evolving self-image.

Even less self-critical, she acknowledged. Still, she had not yet come to grips with fear. It was such a lonely battle! But it was one she had to win before reclaiming her life, Katy thought fiercely. A life with Thomas, she reminded herself whenever darkness threatened to overwhelm her. And on this gray, dreary morning, everything seemed devoid of sunlight.

She was crying again. And suddenly it didn't matter that she was afraid. Right now, in this familiar bedroom whose very walls were patterned with precious memories, only Thomas mattered. No one else could ever fill this aching emptiness.

No one.

She needed him, fiercely, passionately, joyously. The latter realization shocked her. Had she changed that much, that she could take joy in needing someone?

Caution immediately kicked in a warning. Ignoring it, Katy surged to her feet and hurried to her bedroom.

With each step, her need for Thomas Logan became more intense. She could actually *feel* her heart throwing off its shackles, Katy thought delightedly. By the time she reached the telephone, her decision was made.

She would live with Thomas Logan for as long as fate permitted. And she would glory in the living, Katy affirmed her heart's wisdom.

"Welcome to Seattle," the pretty flight attendant said. Katy missed the rest of her spiel. She was here, she was finally *here!* The plane had landed and was now taxiing down the runway, ending an uneventful, routine flight. She released the tattered magazine from her frozen grip, thinking ruefully that she ought to buy the airline a new one.

She hadn't expected flying to be easy, and it wasn't. Terror, nausea, incipient panic, all coalesced to form a single, powerful enemy she'd had to fight moment by moment. Using the deep-breathing exercises Thomas had taught her had helped, but not enough. She had snatched at any distraction her first-class fare offered, watching a movie, chatting with her fellow passengers, reading without comprehension. When she was close to losing it completely, she'd immersed her airsick self in memories of Thomas. The incomparable wonder of their lovemaking. The sweetness of his smile, the bold mischief in his grin. His rock-solid steadiness.

As the plane rolled to a stop, she took her first easy breath of the day. The anticipation fizzing in her blood was more exhilarating than any champagne. Thomas would be waiting at the gate!

She had called him last night.

I'm coming home, Thomas!

I knew you would, I knew it! You'll be okay, Katy.
You'll be fine, my love. You're not afraid of the plane,
you're not even afraid of flying. What you fear is crash-
ing, and that's not going to happen. Trust me, it's not...

Well, she had trusted him and now here she was, rushing to meet him, her eyes frantically searching, and then
finding him. There, that tall, dark-haired man, mouth
laughing, blue gaze warming her from head to toe. Then
she was in his arms, held tightly against his heart, and for
several enchanted minutes, the rest of the world vanished.

There was only Thomas. Her hands knew him, her lips,
her soft, boneless body. Even her soul knew this one man
above all others. She nestled her head against his shoulder
with a long, sweet sigh.

"I love you, Thomas Logan," she murmured.

"I love you, Katy Lawrence," he said huskily.

Thomas figured he was as close to rapture as a man can
come in public. She filled all his senses; he was totally
oblivious to the people surging around them.

He had known from the first that she would be his. But
he'd had to go against all his instincts and let her leave him
before they could be together. It was the toughest thing
he'd ever done. And he would have to do it again and
again, he reminded himself. To keep her, he had to set her
free. Only in that way would she be content to live within
the circle of their love.

At length she drew back far enough to laugh up at him
in joyous communion. "I did it, Thomas! Oh God, I really did it! I got on that plane by myself and I flew by myself..." She paused to snatch a breath.

"And you've come home," he said deeply.

She looked at him searchingly.

He met her gaze and forgot all about breathing. Then her mouth curved into a smile that warmed him inside and out.

"I've come home," she agreed.

"Where you belong."

Katy grinned and tilted her chin. "Now don't get cocky, Thomas," she warned. "My wings aren't all that clipped, you know!"

His husky laugh boomed out. Their voices weaving an intimate rhapsody, they walked from the terminal hand in hand.

*   *   *   *   *

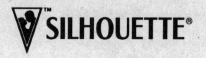

™SILHOUETTE®

Tempting...Tantalising...Terrifying!

Strangers
in the night

Three spooky love stories in one compelling
volume by three masters of the genre:

Dark Journey by Anne Stuart
Catching Dreams by Chelsea Quinn Yarbro
Beyond Twilight by Maggie Shayne

Available: July 1997   Price: £4.99

SILHOUETTE Desire

COMING NEXT MONTH

TALLCHIEF'S BRIDE   Cait London

Man of the Month

The legend said that when a Tallchief placed the ring on the right woman's finger, he would capture true love. Talia Petrovna had gone to the ends of the earth to find Calum Tallchief's ring—but was a woman like her truly fated to be his bride?

A BRIDE FOR ABEL GREENE   Cindy Gerard

Northern Lights Brides

Mail-order bride Mackenzie Kincaid had prepared herself for a loveless marriage to Abel Greene. Now Abel was hesitant; he wanted out of the deal. If Mackenzie wanted to stay wedded, she *had* to seduce her husband!

LOVERS ONLY   Christine Pacheco

Workaholic Clay Landon was so caught up in securing the future that he'd neglected the present—and his wife, Catherine. Could Clay win her back and fulfil her dreams of raising his children?

ROXY AND THE RICH MAN   Elizabeth Bevarly

The Family McCormick

Wealthy businessman Spencer Melbourne hired private investigator Roxy Matheny to find his long-lost twin. Roxy knew she was in over her head—she could give him what he needed professionally, but what about more *personalized* services?

CITY GIRLS NEED NOT APPLY   Rita Rainville

Rugged single-father Mac Ryder knew that city girl Kathryn Wainwright wasn't prepared for the dangers of Wyoming. However, Kathryn knew that the confirmed bachelor was really the one in danger—of settling down with her!

REBEL'S SPIRIT   Susan Connell

Raleigh Hanlon hadn't seen the mischievous Rebecca Barnett in ten years, but now she was home again. Her zest for life had captivated him and he'd stopped even trying to keep her—and his imagination—under control!

COMING NEXT MONTH FROM

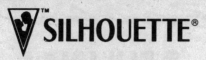

Sensation

A thrilling mix of passion, adventure and drama

AT THE MIDNIGHT HOUR Alicia Scott
MUMMY'S HERO Audra Adams
MAN WITHOUT A MEMORY Maura Seger
MEGAN'S MATE Nora Roberts

Intrigue

Danger, deception and desire

GUARDED MOMENTS Cassie Miles
BULLETPROOF HEART Sheryl Lynn
EDGE OF ETERNITY Jasmine Cresswell
NO WAY OUT Tina Vasilos

Special Edition

Satisfying romances packed with emotion

MUM FOR HIRE Victoria Pade
THE FATHER NEXT DOOR Gina Wilkins
A RANCH FOR SARA Sherryl Woods
RUGRATS AND RAWHIDE Peggy Moreland
A FAMILY WEDDING Angela Benson
THE WEDDING GAMBLE Muriel Jensen

ERICA SPINDLER

Bestselling Author of *Forbidden Fruit*

FORTUNE

BE CAREFUL WHAT YOU WISH FOR...
IT JUST MIGHT COME TRUE

Skye Dearborn's wishes seem to be coming true, but will Skye's new life prove to be all she's dreamed of—or a nightmare she can't escape?

"A high adventure of love's triumph over twisted obsession."

—*Publishers Weekly*

"Give yourself plenty of time, and enjoy!"

—*Romantic Times*

**AVAILABLE IN PAPERBACK
FROM JULY 1997**

JASMINE CRESSWELL

Internationally-acclaimed Bestselling Author

SECRET SINS

The rich are different—they're deadly!

Judge Victor Rodier is a powerful and
dangerous man. At the age of twenty-seven,
Jessica Marie Pazmany is confronted with
terrifying evidence that her real name is
Liliana Rodier. A threat on her life prompts
Jessica to seek an appointment with her
father—a meeting she may live to regret.

**AVAILABLE IN PAPERBACK
FROM JULY 1997**

Bureau de Change

How would you like to win a year's supply of Silhouette® books? Well you can and they're FREE! Simply complete the competition below and send it to us by 31st January 1998. The first five correct entries picked after the closing date will each win a year's subscription to the Silhouette series of their choice. What could be easier?

1.	Lira	Sweden	____
2.	Franc	U.S.A.	____
3.	Krona	Sth. Africa	____
4.	Escudo	Spain	____
5.	Deutschmark	Austria	____
6.	Schilling	Greece	____
7.	Drachma	Japan	____
8.	Dollar	India	____
9.	Rand	Portugal	4
10.	Peseta	Germany	____
11.	Yen	France	____
12.	Rupee	Italy	____

C7G

Please turn over for details of how to enter...

How to enter...

It's that time of year again when most people like to pack their suitcases and head off on holiday to relax. That usually means a visit to the Bureau de Change... Overleaf there are twelve foreign countries and twelve currencies which belong to them but unfortunately they're all in a muddle! All you have to do is match each currency to its country by putting the number of the currency on the line beside the correct country. One of them is done for you! Don't forget to fill in your name and address in the space provided below and pop this page in a envelope (you don't even need a stamp) and post it today. Hurry competition ends 31st January 1998.

Silhouette Bureau de Change Competition
FREEPOST, Croydon, Surrey, CR9 3WZ
EIRE readers send competition to PO Box 4546, Dublin 24.

Please tick the series you would like to receive if you are a winner
Sensation™ ❏ Intrigue™ ❏ Desire™ ❏ Special Edition™❏

Are you a Reader Service™ Subscriber?   Yes ❏   No ❏

Ms/Mrs/Miss/Mr_____
(BLOCK CAPS PLEASE)

Address_____

_____

_____ Postcode_____

(I am over 18 years of age)